"FADING BLUE SKIES"

By Kevin Rice

Printing – Edwards Brothers Malloy, Ann Arbor Michigan

ISBN - 978-0-692-70052-5

The author thanks: **Jesus Christ** for all that You have given me and encouraged me with to honor You and our Heavenly Father. May all I am continue to be all You want me to be. **My editors – Rita and Traci**, hopefully this book was easier to edit. Your help and encouragement is deeply appreciated. **'Maggie's Family'** – Thank you for all you have done. You have been priceless in my life. **My family**, thank you for all your love and support. You mean more to me than I can ever show.

FADING BLUE SKIES

This book is dedicated to '*Mr.* and *Mrs. Nelson*'

"Do not let the crutch of an addiction be the anchor that brings you down"
~~Kevin Rice

CHAPTER ONE

Love is a mystery for the ages. It is a story that is as old as time. Can it be told any differently? Is it so familiar that no one really wants to hear another one? Unlikely. Love stories tug at the heart. They make the reader feel like they are not alone in the world. No matter what story is told and no matter how familiar it can be, there is always someone who knows exactly what the character is going through, something to bring those two lives together, the characters and the readers.

Love comes in many forms. On one hand, we have the greatest expression and example of love from God. It was out of love that He created us. It was that same love that made Jesus come to earth. He was born to show us that God was still with us. He taught us many things. In Matt 22:37 he taught us that the greatest commandment is to love, "love the Lord your God with all your heart, with all your soul, and with all your mind." He went on to teach us to "love your neighbor as yourself." Straight from the mouth of our Savior is this commandment, the commandment that we should love.

In John 15:12-13, Jesus taught us, 'that you love one another as I have loved you. Greater love has no one than this, than to lay down one's life for his friends." Jesus was never one to just stand around and preach words. He would always allow His actions to back up His words. To prove this, He walked to the cross on His own accord. He suffered beatings, ridicule, and eventually death to pay the penalty for our sins. He did this for His friends, those that do whatever He commands us (John 15:14). The story of His love for us didn't end at the cross. It was evident in the empty tomb and in His resurrection. We will also see it fully in His glorious appearing when He returns. How many of us can say that we have ever loved anyone to the extent that we would die for them? How many of us would do it for someone that was beating us? My guess, not many.

This kind of love has no equal.

It is pure.

It is unconditional.

The best thing is, this kind of love is a gift given freely from God to those willing to accept it. Even though many have tried to duplicate this kind of love, it has never been equaled. In reality, it never could ever be. However, because of its genuineness and purity, it never hurts to try. A love like that is a goal worth striving for.

On the other hand, the love we share as humans is a different story. It can be the source of the greatest joy that any of us have ever experienced. It can also be what causes us the most pain. Most search for real love because we know a hint of the joy it can bring. As true as that statement is, we spend more time hiding from it because no one wants to have to experience the pain that a broken love can bring.

Love has built many kingdoms and conversely it has brought many kingdoms to ruin. It has made mankind soar to heights that nothing else in the world could have. It has also been the source of the downfall of many.

Throughout history, everyone has searched for love at some point in their lives. Most have been lucky enough to find it or some semblance of it that is. Even though some have been fortunate enough to experience the joy of finding someone to love, it is an almost undisputable fact that everyone that has ever walked the face of this earth, in some form or another, knows the pain of a love that has been lost. Sadly, love is usually right in front of us but rarely seen. We expect it to be revealed in some Hollywood fashion, like sky rockets, or two lovers running towards each other in the rain, or some other unrealistic way. We want it only by our expectations of it and very rarely does love approach us this way. When it doesn't present itself in such a way, most believe it isn't real and end up pushing it away. It is usually a lot more subtle. It quietly enters our life and slowly fills our very being. Until one day, the person you didn't think had much of a place in your heart becomes the very reason why your heart is beating. That is the true and genuine love we search for.

Too few ever find this.

Even fewer actually appreciate it when it is there.

That's the way it was for Christian Emerson. He had searched his whole life for true love. He was a romantic. He believed in chivalry. He believed in unconditional love. He believed that even a small amount of unconditional love was worth far more than all the riches in the entire world. Not the romantic movie style of true love but the genuine love that lasts not only through the good times, but also through the bad. Not the shallow kind of 'love' people sometimes mistake as genuine.

Christian had moved to Scotland a couple of years ago, as much in part from running from the pain of his past as it was, to hopefully start on a brighter future. The pain of life can make us do things that many would think of as irrational and moving to Scotland seemed like a very irrational thing at the time. Now, after being there for the last two years, it turned out to be the best decision he had ever made. His past in the United States seemed like a completely different life now. A life of pain and heartache. A life that he hoped he would never have to live again.

Like anyone that has ever wanted genuine love, he didn't see it when it arrived in his life. It's funny how people will search for something, yet the last place they look is right in front of them. It was that way for Christian when he first met this interesting woman from across the pond.

~~~~~~~~~~

Christian Emerson was in his early thirties when he moved to Scotland just over two years ago. He grew up just west of Detroit in a town whose claim to fame was the birth of the auto industry. As much as his father had hoped that he would follow in his footsteps and be an engineer,

Christian had other plans. This started a rift between him and his father that, over the years, never healed. He had two younger sisters but was the only son and according to his father, was nothing more than a big disappointment. This bothered Christian during his teenage years but as he grew older, he knew there was nothing he could do to make his father be proud of him. So he lived his life trying to serve others. He hoped that one day his father would see the good he was trying to do and be proud of him anyway. This was a hope that Christian realized would never come true. Deep in his heart he was saddened by this but refused to let it change his path in life. He believed that what he wanted to do would honor his Heavenly Father and therefore that was the path he put himself on, even though his earthly father despised him for it.

After high school, Christian decided to go to college to get his BSN, Bachelor of Science in Nursing. He was just over six feet tall and being a former hockey player, he was still in pretty good shape. To look at him though, no one would have ever thought he would go into nursing as a profession. He stayed focused and completed his degree. He was anxious to get to work as soon as he could. After college he moved south to Toledo Ohio and landed a job in the emergency center of one of the level 1 trauma hospitals in the area. Although his professional life was moving along well, his personal life was the complete opposite. While on his lunch break one day at work, he found himself reading a magazine. As he was flipping through the pages, he stumbled across an advertisement looking for experienced RN's to work as travel nurses. He never thought about it until that very moment but that one moment was all it took. After his break, he asked his supervisor to write a recommendation letter. When he went home after his shift, he took his chance and applied for the job and narrowed his request to Scotland. As far back as he could remember, on the entire planet, that little section on the north end of Britain was the only place he wanted to see. He said a quiet prayer that this was where God wanted him to be.

To his surprise, it worked out in his favor. The travel RN agency interviewed him first and not long after, the Royal Infirmary of Loch Grádh, located near Edinburgh flew him out for a second interview. Within a month, Christian Emerson was on his way to a new life. One he was heading to with a happy heart. It was the first time, in a long time, that his heart felt happy about anything. His contract was only supposed to last for six months. Two years later, he was still there, with no intention of heading back to the US anytime soon.

He stayed for many reasons. He stayed because he enjoyed his job immensely. Christian was good with his patients. His supervisor was so impressed with his way of dealing with patients that after his 6 month contract was finished, he was asked to stay on. Christian was happy to stay. Aside from the fact that he really liked his job, he stayed there because there was also just too much pain in his past, back in the US, that he couldn't even face the thought of it.

Although Christian worked at the hospital about half way between the big city and the eastern coastline, he chose to stay in a rented flat in the little town of Loch Grádh. Loch Grádh was a small fishing village about a 20 minute train ride northwest of Edinburgh. There was a history in this town. Even though it was a gateway port for people arriving from Europe and invaders arriving from Norway, the town never really grew. There was a lineage of a few families that had withstood time. On any given day, though, there was an average of 1500 people living in that little town.

Christian had spent his first week in Scotland settling into his new surroundings. The following two weeks, working almost every day, was spent at the Infirmary in orientation and training. It felt like a long time before he had a few days off in a row. He was the type of person who would plunge deep into his work and did everything there was to help make the new hospital a better healthcare setting in the eyes of their patients. It was something he learned from a sermon by his favorite pastor, when he said that when you work, have the mindset that you are working directly for Jesus. However you would work for Him, is how you should work for any other employer. This helped make Christian a great nurse and well liked by his patients and peers.

When he finally did have some time off, he spent it exploring the new area that he was now calling home. One day he came across a castle, named after the family line that had lived there for over 800 years. There were still some ruins on the property, but the main building seemed to be in good shape. There was also a smaller, newer building on the north side of the property about one hundred yards from the castle. This, he learned later, was where the family lived. They still owned the land there and all that was on it. Yet it was a distant relative that managed the castle and all the tours that went through every day.

Not only was it the beauty of Scotland that he had seen in numerous photos on the internet that intrigued him, it was also the history. This castle had its fair share of history. So he returned there every day over the next week. He wasn't sure if it was the history or the beauty of the landscape that drew him in, but whatever it was, Stewart Castle and the loch had a hold on him. On the third day, he overheard one of the tour guides saying that he was retiring and that his position there would be available. He immediately poke to the manager and by the end of the week, Christian was working there as a tour guide. He was paid a modest wage but Christian so enjoyed this job, that he would've done it for free. What he learned and shared with the visitors that came through, was worth it. The entire area was unlike anything he had ever seen or experienced back in the United States. Within a month of being in Scotland he knew he made the right decision to go. The happiness on their faces made doing the job priceless.

Overall, his life in Scotland was going well. He hadn't been to the US in over two years and that was fine with him. All the painful memories he had left behind now all seemed like a bad dream that was slowly fading. Christian was in no rush to go back. He wasn't that close with his two sisters. They had both married and moved away from Michigan as soon as they could. They started their own families and rarely kept in touch with him. They had their occasional chat on the phone, but even those had been getting more and more rare. Christian's parents divorced when he was a toddler and he had spent only a handful of days with his mother since then. Of course, the topper was, that since he was a complete disappointment to his father, Christian had given up making any effort to reach him on any level, especially since in the last conversation they had, his dad said that he didn't care if Christian ever called again. It was obvious that his father didn't care, because it had been over 7 years since they had spoken. So, the only son of Mr. Emerson gave him exactly what he wanted, a life without ever hearing from him again. It was sad that after 30 years, this was the life that Christian had with his family. However, if it wasn't for the disconnect in his personal life, Christian wouldn't have even thought to actually leave his home and go as far away as he did. In some respects, it may have been a bittersweet decision, but it was turning out to be the best he had ever made, since it was less bitter and much more sweet.

And then there was the other reason he left. The reason that caused even more pain in his heart than the dysfunction that he had with his family. Pain that had been such a deep part of his life that at times it felt like it would never go away. It was a pain that with every breath, it felt like the knife was twisting deeper and deeper. His new life helped to ease it but the constant reminder was there. Like a shadow that in his heart and mind that would never leave.

CHAPTER TWO

It was early spring on the east coast of Scotland. There was a chill in the air that indicated that no matter how much the sun tried to warm the air, winter wasn't going to give up without a fight. With the help of the rising sun, that morning winter was going to lose the battle, just as it always did. The budding flowers and trees were a strong indication as well, that spring would win and winter would soon start its long hibernation.

Margaret Elizabeth Greene woke to the sun shining in through the window of the cottage she was renting in Scotland. Last night was the first restful sleep that she had had in weeks. Margaret arrived in Scotland just over a month ago. When her mom asked why she wanted to go in the middle of winter, she had a very easy answer for her. She had only planned to stay for a few months and told her mom that she wanted to experience the change of seasons. If all went according to plan, she would catch the end of winter, all of spring and then the beginning of summer before she was scheduled to go back to the United States.

It had taken her very little time to get used to the change of scenery. This was definitely different from where she grew up in Toledo Ohio. Her home town in northwest Ohio was considered a smaller town in comparison to other cities across the pond. Being over here took some getting used to and the openness and beauty were nothing compared to anything back home. Every once in a while she was homesick but the more she started to venture out and explore, the more comfortable she was beginning to feel. Things were getting better and she was starting to enjoy being there and missed home less and less.

She reluctantly climbed out of bed, walked over to the window and slid the curtains open so she could look out. Mist was rising as the sun was starting to warm the ground. She took in a deep breath of the warming air and then smiled as she stepped away from the window and headed to the kitchen to make a cup of hot tea. Back home in Toledo, she rarely drank tea. But here, in the eastern hillsides of Scotland, on this brisk but sunny morning, it just seemed like the natural thing to do.

This morning, instead of eating her breakfast at the small little table in the kitchenette of the cottage, Margaret decided to take her tea and two slices of toast out on the porch and watch as the day was waking up with her. Maggie, as her mom called her ever since she could remember, was in good spirits that morning. It seemed, at that moment, all the worries she held so tightly to didn't exist. In that moment, she felt a freedom she couldn't ever remember feeling before.

As she sat on the porch, Maggie looked out across the field. She wrapped a blanket around her petite frame. Her long blond hair was pulled back in a pony tail that was tied with a plaid ribbon and hung over the edge of her blanket. The short cobblestone sidewalk just outside the front door, led out to the gate, across the small road and out into the field right across the way. The field was filled with wild flowers that were starting to bloom, which was one of the draws to this particular cottage when she was looking for a place to stay. The advertisement of the cottage bragged about the beauty of the wild flowers and the active wild life. The deer and other wildlife didn't seem to mind her being there and she enjoyed watching them. Even though Maggie couldn't see it herself, there was a peace about her that made most people attracted to her. That peace was finally beginning to find its way into her heart.

The wild life around the cottage seemed to sense that peace as well. That morning, like most days, the animals had no problem wandering near the porch where she now sat. As a fawn wandered close to the porch, a doe raised her head to keep a protective watch over her little one. Sensing no trouble, the protective mother deer went back to looking for her own food. Maggie didn't pay any attention to the mother deer. Her attention was focused on the fawn as she wandered up right next to the porch. Maggie stretched her arm out to offer her a piece of toast that she had picked up off the plate on the side table. In that moment, nothing existed in the world other than the two of them. A gentle breeze blew across Maggie's hair causing a few strands to fall across her face. She didn't even notice as her attention was still on the baby deer leaning forward about to nibble at the toast being offered. Maggie didn't move a muscle as the trusting fawn finished her breakfast and then looked up to see if there was more. The doe had moved to within 20 feet of her little one but still, not sensing any danger, she just continued eating her own breakfast. The fawn waited only a moment before realizing no more food would be offered. After a quick glance at Maggie, the little deer joined its mother who was looking for her own food to eat.

As Maggie went back to eating the small piece of toast she had left, she could hear the water rushing of the rocks in the nearby stream. The serenity of the area was helping Maggie to understand that she needed to let go of those struggles that she held onto. The stream was a short walk from the cottage and she thought that if she had time later that day she would take a walk to the waters edge. She still hadn't grown tired of looking at the surrounding beauty and all it had to offer and was enjoying her time exploring.

She sat taking in all that was around her. Her thoughts drifted, as she started to think about the history of the area and wondered what stories the surrounding hills would tell if they could talk. She wasn't far from Stewart Castle. According to her mother, way back in their ancestry, they were Stewarts and this castle had been a part of that history. That is why she had chosen to come here and do a thesis on her family for her MA degree in English. This part of the world was a long way from where she grew up in Toledo, Ohio. It was a long way from Ann Arbor Michigan where she attended the university and would hopefully soon receive the degree she had worked so long on. Once completed, she would eventually teach. Maybe I could teach here, she thought.

She didn't want to think about all of that right now.

She wanted to enjoy the moment and enjoy the view. She struggled to sit still at times, well most times actually. She always felt like she had to be on the run to 'do things'. It never mattered what those things were, as long as she didn't have to sit still. Being here, she had to force herself to slow down. It was difficult at first, but in the month since she had arrived, she was slowly teaching herself to do just that. So there, in that moment, she sat drinking her tea and enjoying the beautiful view of the rolling hills, the awakening hills, and shimmering water that was around her.

Maggie wasn't sure how long she had been sitting there but soon realized that she had better get ready for her day. She was supposed to meet with Christian Emerson at 11:30. They were going to have a quick lunch before heading over to the castle to do more research. Christian had told Maggie that today they were going to discuss the history behind the area surrounding the castle. Something that really excited her.

~~~~~~~~~~

When she was finally ready, she raced out of the cottage and out to the rented car parked on the side. The fawn and doe had moved to about 50 yards from where they had been only 30 minutes prior. Maggie stopped to glance at them. She would have stayed that way if it hadn't been for the alarm on her cell phone that went off reminding her that she was already supposed to be at the restaurant where her friend was waiting.

The drive to the little town of Loch Grádh was only about ten minutes away from the cottage. It was a quiet drive through the lowland hills. Maggie drove through the occasional patch of mist as it was rising up the hill side. To the right, off in the distance, she noticed a stag running across an open field. Even though she was running a little late, she slowed her vehicle just a bit to watch as the stag made one leap and then disappeared into the edge of the woods. She marveled at the way the wildlife was so visible here. Back home, at the most she would see the occasional deer as she walked through the local metro park. She finely reached the pub and quickly got out of her car to head inside. Her last thought before walking in was that she was happy the fawn ate most of her breakfast. She was very hungry as she opened the doors to the pub.

Chapter Three

By the time Maggie had made it to the pub, Christian was already there. She really liked this establishment. There was a lot of history in this area and the pub was no exception. She had done a little bit of research prior to departing on this little adventure to Scotland. When she was looking for a place that she would be able to sit and enjoy a good meal, The Pipers was at the top of the list of 'Must Sees' while in this grand country. After her first visit there, she could see why it was so highly rated.

As she walked in, Maggie noticed Christian sitting at a dark wooden table along the far wall, across from the door. The regulars, sitting at the bar to the right of the door, looked up and greeted her as she made her way to where

Christian was sitting. They were a fun group of people. The more Maggie frequented the pub, the more familiar they were getting with each other. Listening to them greet her in their thick Scottish accent, made her smile every time.

On the opposite wall from the bar was a large stone fireplace. Maggie wasn't sure if the information she had found on the Scottish Travel website was accurate, but she had read that this fireplace and part of the actual bar was the oldest part of this entire building. At one point in the middle of the 1700's, a fire in the kitchen spread to the dining area and consumed most of the building. The stone fireplace and the top of the bar were about the only thing that had survived. The owners did not want to let that defeat them so they rebuilt the pub around the fireplace. They even used some of the original ceiling beams to rebuild the bar. Once the repairs were completed, they continued to provide weary travelers with a tasty meal, a refreshing glass of mead, and a welcoming place for them to rest their weary bones before continuing on to places further away. When the time came, the owners passed the pub on to their children. This continued for generation after generation up to and including the current owner, Angus Donnchaidh.

The crackle and pop of the wood burning in the fireplace brought back memories of her parent's home in Toledo. Their family had spent many summer evenings out in the back yard around a fire pit that her dad had built. It was just a little one but all the time they spent out there was priceless in her eyes. Their conversations, that would frequently jump from subject to subject, always brought them closer as a family. Maggie stopped briefly, taking in the smell of the fire burning across the room, then continued to the table where she could see Christian waiting.

"Hi Maggie," Angus said from behind the long oaken bar as she walked past him. "Will ya be having your usual diet cola this fine morning?" Hidden just underneath the smell coming from the fireplace was the faint smell of fresh baked bread coming from the kitchen and that made her stomach grumble just a bit as it was wanting to get a taste of the good food she had already grown accustomed to.

She smiled as he said this in his thick Scottish accent. It was actually in this very restaurant that she had met Christian when she first arrived in town. She had wanted to get out of the cottage and become familiar with the area, so she had decided to finally visit the local eatery she had read about. At the end of her first week, she ventured out to have some dinner. When she walked in that day for the first time, she had met Angus and couldn't understand a word he was saying. Christian, who had been sitting there enjoying his own dinner, stood up and helped her 'interpret' what Angus was saying. That day Christian and Maggie had started a friendship that has grown steadily stronger ever since.

"Yes please. I am very thirsty today so I'll have a glass of water, as well," she replied without breaking stride on her way to her waiting friend. It was barely thirty yards from the front door to the table where Christian was sitting. He had met Maggie almost a dozen times here for a meal in order for them to work on her paper. With each time she walked in, it had taken Maggie longer and longer to make that walk. The patrons were always happy to see her sparkling green eyes as they smiled. The more comfortable she was becoming in that restaurant, the more she talked to everyone sitting there when she walked in.

She made her way over to where Christian was sitting. "I'm sorry for being late." She said with a sigh as she set her purse and back pack on the chair next to the one she chose to sit on. She took her jacket off and hung it on the back of her chair across from him and sat down with another deep sigh.

Angus walked up and set her diet soda and water on the table as Maggie was adjusting her chair up to the table. "Will ya be eating anything today, Lassie?"

"I think I will have a bowl of that delicious stew that you had last week if you have that on the menu today."

"Aye, good choice," being a man of few words, Angus departed back to the kitchen leaving Maggie and Christian to themselves.

"Maggie, don't be stressed about being late." He tried to ease her tension a bit. He was smiling, enjoying her company more with each passing visit.

"I know but I feel bad you had to wait for me."

"I only just arrived myself. So there is nothing to worry about." Christian was from the US but the longer he had been in Scotland the more it seemed like the memories from the US were fading and his new home was taking root. Every once in a while Maggie could detect a little of the Scottish brogue working its way into his speech.

She let a smile slip out. She knew she had the tendency to let little things bother her a little too much. She just didn't want to be a nuisance to anyone. She took him at his word that he didn't feel put out and decided to let things be. This was something new for her. She realized that Scotland was having its effect on her as well. It was something that she was starting to grow accustomed to, and it didn't bother her one little bit.

"How was your morning?" Christian asked, trying to change the subject to something a little lighter. He asked that every time and Maggie was awed by his genuineness that he cared enough to make sure she was happy and felt at home.

"Are you enjoying your cottage?" He had never been there but without ever telling her, he was looking forward to seeing it. Maggie had described it almost every time they were together but as of yet, had not invited him to come see it. He was getting to know her well and knew that it was because that place was her sanctuary, the place where she was able to be herself and feel safe.

"I am. It is very peaceful." She paused for a moment, and then added, "I sat out on the porch to drink a cup of tea as I watched the day wake up. I tried to imagine all the history that these hills could tell, if they could speak." She was going to tell him about what happened when the fawn was sharing her breakfast but decided to keep that one just to herself. She was thankful to Jesus for that moment that seemed to bring her closer to Him.

As Christian was about to make a comment, he was distracted by Angus approaching the table with their food; fish and chips for Christian and stew and bread for Maggie. Angus hadn't asked Maggie if she wanted bread, but Angus read his customers very well. After that first night she was in there, Angus knew that Maggie enjoyed her bread more than anything else. He believed that the only reason she ordered the stew today was to get more of the fresh baked bread his cook had taken out of the oven not even 20 minutes earlier.

CHAPTER FOUR

While they started on their lunch, Maggie and Christian made small talk. The topics ranged from her life in America to his life in Scotland. She talked about her university days, her family in Toledo and her sister in Los Angeles. She asked him about his job at the Infirmary. For the most part though, Christian sat and listened to his friend. Maggie would stop every once in awhile to mention that she was still shocked that they were from the same area of northwest Ohio and that they had never known each other. There was a seven year difference in their ages so they hung out with different crowds. Then she would continue on with another thought until it came back around to their connection to that part of the world.

It amazed Christian to think of the history that each person on the planet carried in their hearts. It was always easy for him to see just how comfortable someone was with him by how much that person was willing to share. It served him well in his job and he realized it was the way that God wanted everyone to treat each other, with love. It was a good show of trust when someone was willing to open up and, sitting there in The Pipers Pub in Scotland, it was obvious that Maggie was growing more comfortable with Christian. Every time they talked, she opened up a little more. After each encounter with her, he was growing more fond of her.

They were about half way through their meals when Christian let his thoughts drift for a minute. He had found that Maggie had been very shy at first, not really wanting to open up. So he would chat a little bit until he found a subject that she felt comfortable talking about and then he would slowly ease back on what he was saying just to listen to her speak. He had begun to grow more and more fascinated while listening to her talk. Once she felt comfortable, she seemed to be able to talk for hours. Christian would just sit and listen to her open up, fascinated at the stories she told. When it seemed like she had exhausted what she wanted to talk about, she would ask questions to get him to open up a little more. He found it more interesting to hear about her life, so he didn't talk much about himself. He took a drink of his water to bring him back to the moment.

"So I was wondering, as I was sitting on the porch this morning drinking my tea, about the history of the lake near here. Where did the name come from? Why is this area named Loch Grádh?" She said trying to bring the conversation back to what she really wanted to talk about.

As he was about to speak, the juke box in the corner

between the end of the bar and the restroom started to play a song. There was a plethora of songs that could have played but the random song that started was, coincidentally enough, a version of 'Scotland the Brave' that Christian really enjoyed. It was by a musician who seemed to only write songs about Scotland and did a great job at that. Since arriving in Scotland and hearing a few of his songs, Christian added all of the musicians CDs to his own collection and listened to them when he could. Maggie could tell Christian was listening to the jukebox and reached for her diet soda. She took a drink as she watched him. Even though he was from the Midwest part of the United States, he was clearly drawn to this country. It was difficult to explain but she could definitely see it.

"My apologies," he said.

"No need to apologize."

"Well," he said when the song was over and with a smile forming on his lips, "the story of Loch Grádh is a very interesting story." He began to tell the story that he had learned when he first arrived and had retold and edited countless time to many tourists. It was a story of love. A story that was unlike many had ever heard before.

"Some of the greatest stories ever to have been passed down from one generation to another have a love story at the heart of it, no pun intended." He smiled.

As Christian started, Maggie interrupted and added a quick request before he began his story, "I know you tell an edited version of this during your tour of the castle, but if I may, I would like to hear the lengthy version. That is, if you don't mind taking the time to tell me."

He smiled at her request and instead of giving her a direct answer, he began with the Legend of Loch Grádh.

"Many, many years ago, the king of England was having trouble with the Scottish people."

"How long ago does this story take place?" Maggie interjected quickly. At first Christian took her question as her not wanting to listen. Then remembering that she was very inquisitive and he dismissed the thought. He was learning that in order for Maggie to understand something, she needed as much of the details as possible.

"Well, the legend, as it has been told to me by members of the family and what I could find in my research of local history, began in the late 14th century." Christian was smiling at how intrigued Maggie was and he had barely begun with the story. "Remember though, like most legends, especially one that has lasted this long, the actual events may be somewhat sketchy and somewhat embellished."

"Many years ago, the king of England was having trouble with the Scottish people." He repeated and then continued, "the king was wanting to have control over the whole island of Britain."

She sat listening intently as he continued his story. She took a sip of her diet soda and a small bite of the warm bread that she had spread soft, fresh butter and fruit preserves on. Her bowl of half eaten stew was still sitting on the table nearby.

"Despite his greed and desire to rule the whole island, the king was failing at the task because his castle was in the southern part of England. It was difficult to move supplies and an army the size he needed, that far away. It was also difficult because the people in the north didn't want to be ruled by a king that was as ruthless and greedy as the current king was known to be. However that part of the story will have to be for another time. The only point of bringing it up now is that if he had been a better king, he may have had more support from those he ruled over."

Christian paused for a moment to take a sip of his water and then continued.

"The king transplanted noblemen and their family members from the central part of the country to lands and estates in the northern part of England, near York. He even placed a few of his very loyal nobles up there as well. However, the more of his followers that he placed up there, the more supplies he needed to take care of them, until their own farm lands began to produce enough food. In the southern part of the country, the greedy king tried to impose more taxes on the people, but they had nothing to give. The wars across the channel, that this king kept them in, were bleeding them dry to the point that they didn't have enough to feed their own families. However, that didn't stop the king from taking what they had anyway. If the farmers on the king's land wouldn't give what they were 'taxed' to give, they were either run off or killed and then the king would replace them with someone more loyal to the crown than themselves."

"So when the people were unable to pay, he had them killed and took their lands. He replaced them with more nobles loyal to him. It was a vicious circle that seemed to have no end."

"Well so far this doesn't sound like much of a love story," Maggie muttered with a smile.

Christian smiled back. "Well it doesn't start out that way, but be patient. It does get better."

They both took a bite of what remained on their plates. After another quick drink of water, Christian pushed his plate of half eaten food away and then continued on with his story.

"One area the king was having a big problem with was this area of Scotland. The Scottish were alienated when a Roman emperor built a wall in northern England. As much as the emperor was trying to upset the Scottish with this, they were not all that mad about it. They wanted to be a country all their own and they didn't want to be ruled by that or any other tyrant that was bent only on dominating the world, or at the very least their little corner of it."

"So the King of England decided that he would transplant one of his closest nobleman right here in what is now called Stewart Castle. The nobleman that he chose was a God fearing man named Audric. Audric is an old Gaelic name which means wise ruler. It was a name that seemed to suit him because he was well liked by those he was instructed to rule over."

"He was well liked by the people because he was fair and just. This was different from the way the king he served ruled. The nobleman's knight guard that served as protection in the area liked him. He was one of the rare nobles that actually earned the respect of those in his area and did his best to keep it that way."

Maggie was practically sitting on the edge of her seat. She had been holding her glass of diet soda but hadn't taken a drink. She was intrigued with the history and imagery unfolding before her as Christian retold the legend.

It made Christian smile because he hadn't even reached the interesting part. "He and his wife had four children, two sons and two daughters. His oldest, a son William, stayed in the south with the king as a part of the knights serving the crown. His youngest, also a son Edward, wasn't old enough to join the knights but told his father frequently that once he was old enough, he would follow in his brother's footsteps.

This saddened Audric, as the legend goes, because his sons wanted to follow the ruthless, greedy king more than their own father. The nobleman lived his life as a man of God. He knew that he couldn't hold his sons back but, in his heart, he prayed they would see the king for what he was and that their hearts would change."

Maggie finally took a sip of her soda and quietly set her glass back on the table, not wanting to distract Christian as he continued on with his story.

"Audric had two daughters, Denalla and Aileen, and that is where the story really gets to the heart of the matter." Christian watched Maggie smile at the pun.

~~~~~~~~~~~~~

Maggie had long since finished eating, and it was at that point that they both realized that they had been sitting for almost two hours. They were starting to get restless sitting at the table, so they decided to finish up at The Pipers and head over to the castle grounds so Christian could finish his story.

"We can pick up the story where Audric's oldest daughter Denalla falls in love with Sir Aylwin, one of the knights serving in the nobleman's guard."

"Sounds like a good plan." Maggie excused herself to the restroom after taking another sip of her diet soda. Christian stood and cleaned the tables of the plates, glasses and trash. He usually did this even though Angus had told him many times that he didn't have to. While he did that, he said a quiet prayer that God was with Maggie as he had his suspicions of what was happening with her. Their time together had shown that there might be an eating disorder.

Christian sat and waited, when Maggie returned to the

table. They both put their coats on and made their way out to the car park to where Christian had his car sitting. Maggie suggested that they leave her car at the pub and that they would pick it up after they were done at the castle. They joked and made small talk as they got in the car to drive over to Stewart Castle.

Chapter Five

The clouds were few but had been gathering more when Maggie had walked into The Pipers Pub earlier that day. Now they were starting to clear and the sun was warming the cool spring air. It wasn't a long drive to the castle grounds from where they had eaten their lunch. Maggie and Christian made small talk as they drove through town and headed out onto the narrow country road that led to Stewart Castle. The drive was interrupted briefly when a shepherd they came upon was crossing the road with a large flock of sheep. They sat watching, waiting for him to finish leading the slow animals to their drinking hole at the bottom of the hill.

When the last sheep had crossed, the shepherd in a

long tweed coat, raised his hand in a friendly wave, turned and followed the sheep down the small embankment to a pond where the first of the flock had already reached and were beginning to quench their thirst.

Maggie watched in amazement at this sight. She explained to Christian that she had never seen anyone as patient as he was when being held up in 'traffic' as he had been during the last 20 minutes. She explained that back home, people were very impatient on the road. There would never be sheep walking across the road there but if there were, guaranteed people would be pressing the horn on their car in order to get the sheep to move faster.

"People are a lot more patient here than they are back where I came from in the States as well, as you know of course. People always seem to be in such a big hurry to get anywhere, and it is usually somewhere they complain about having to get to."

Maggie laughed knowing exactly what he was saying. "There is a freeway near my house back home where people will drive 15 miles an hour over the limit. Most of the people I know use that stretch just to go a few exits to get to work, and it is to a job I hear them complain about almost every day." That was the first time Christian had heard her mention anything about her friends back in Ohio. He never talked about his past to her because he didn't want to think about it himself. Maggie however, rarely spoke about her life other than her family and her cats. He could tell that her pets were what she was most proud of. Her face lit up when she spoke of them.

They pulled into the driveway leading up to the castle grounds as Maggie finished sharing memories of her life in Toledo Ohio. This wasn't the first time that Christian had driven Maggie to the castle. The look on her face though was as if she was seeing it for the first time each time they arrived. She told him that it was the history of the place that held her in such intrigue.

He understood what she was referring to. In all the places he lived, he had never seen anything like it until he moved to Scotland. There wasn't anything like this back where he was from. That was part of the reason he took the part time job as a tour guide there. All his life, the time period in human history that this reflected, had always held him in awe.

After he parked his car near the back of the parking lot they got out and then they made their way directly towards the loch. He had taken her through the castle a couple of times, but on that day Christian thought it would be good to walk along the trail near the water. Since that was where the important part of the story took place, it seemed like a logical choice. Maggie walked along side of him, patiently but eagerly waiting for him to continue the legend.

"So where was I?" Christian smiled as he said this, knowing that Maggie was waiting to hear the rest of the story. He knew that she was anxious to hear it not just because it was a part of her thesis paper but also because it was part of her family history. Maggie had told him that her mother had done her own ancestry search and traced their family tree back to this very castle. However, the trail ran cold for her mother and as Maggie told it, her mom was equally excited to hear any continuation of their heritage that the young American was able to find out."

"You were talking about the nobleman's oldest daughter." Maggie reminded him with a smile.

"Oh yeah, her name was Denalla, by the way, her name

means dark haired elfin girl."

Chapter Six

When Maggie and Christian had first arrived at Stewart Castle, they parked at the end of the parking lot, near where he parked when he was on shift to work at the castle. As they walked to toward the loch they were both struck silent. They were not able to determine where the sound was coming from, but the haunting melody from a single bagpiper echoed from the direction of the loch. Bagpipes were an instrument one either loved or hated. They tended to have a sound that not everyone could tolerate. Christian always loved the sound of the pipes. It was an instrument he had always wanted to learn. Listening to it that day with Maggie made that desire even stronger.

The first time Christian had heard the sound of the

mysterious piper he had stopped and listened as it cut through the mist that rolled down the side of the mountain, through the glen and out across the water. The next time he had worked after hearing the piper, he asked his supervisor at the castle what he knew.

"Mostly legends," was all Iain McClellan would say. Christian was unable to get anything else out of his tight lipped boss. Knowing that pressing for anything more would get him nowhere, the American dropped the subject but he did not drop his curiosity. Christian did some of his own research into some of the legends surrounding the castle, but he wasn't able to turn up much. What he did find was a sketchy history that was told to him from those that lived in the area. The American decided that none of it was verifiable and even though he wanted to find an answer, decided to let it go, for the time being.

Maggie looked over as Christian just stared in the direction of the loch. They both stood like that as the haunting melody continued to play. They both could have stood like that for hours listening to the bagpipes as the music seemed to reach, not only into the heart but into the deepest part of the soul.

~~~~~~~~~~~

Once the music stopped and the echo faded, they continued to the pathway that led around the main building, well manicured landscape, and out towards the banks of the loch. It was a fifteen minute walk at a slow pace. They were in no rush so as they took their time, the two enjoyed the beauty of the area. While they walked, Christian continued retelling the Loch Grádh Legend.

"Denalla was a strong woman and this made her father and mother very proud. Audric would be heard frequently saying that he never had to worry about his children because they all knew how to take care of themselves." This drew a smile on Christian's face because Maggie had mentioned once how scared she was to fly to Scotland all by herself, but when he looked at her, he could see the same strength in her that he had heard of Audric's description of Denalla.

"One day, Audric was walking through the courtyard of the castle grounds and he noticed that Denalla was standing with Sir Aylwin, one of Audric's most skilled knights. At first he was furious that the knight would be so bold as to speak with his daughter. It was inappropriate and unheard of. However, his anger faded when he heard his daughter laugh at something the young man had said to her."

Maggie was listening intently as her guide continued on with the story. By that time they had reached the loch and a bench that was near the edge of the water. She motioned for them to sit and nodded to Christian for him to continue his history lesson about the young couple.

"Days and weeks passed and the two were seen with each other whenever they could. They never hid their affection for one another. When Sir Aylwin approached the young lady's father to ask for her hand in marriage, the young woman's father couldn't help but say yes. Audric was extremely impressed that the knight respected not only him, but also his daughter, so much so that he would do such a thing." Christian paused for a moment and then added, "The legend says that the two men walked near the edge of the loch, this loch, right about where we are at right now when the younger man asked for the beautiful Denalla's hand in marriage."

Maggie was all but beaming at this point. She, like most women, enjoyed a good love story and so far, this one was shaping up to be a good one. She couldn't wait to hear the rest of it, secretly hoping that this story had a happy ending.

"Are you enjoying the story so far?"

"I am, but please, don't stop," and that was all Maggie said.

So without any further delay, Christian continued.

"Audric knew that as his daughter grew up and became even more beautiful many more men would try to win her affection. He believed that this young man standing in front of him, next to the loch, was a good man, a worthy suitor, and would treat his daughter well. He had been part of his garrison of knights for the last four years. Sir Aylwin had been respectful and when the times called for it, did his duty and protected the nobleman and his family while, at times, putting his very life in danger."

Christian was about to continue when Maggie started to cough. It was a hacking cough that didn't seem to be producing much phlegm. Maggie placed a handkerchief to her mouth that she had pulled from the front pocket of her back pack. Christian was about to ask how long she had had the cough, his training starting to kick in, when she pulled the cloth away from her mouth. His heart sank when he noticed the red drops in a small circle in the center of the cloth. She crumbled the handkerchief into the palm of her hand. He could tell that she did it in a fast motion hoping that he wouldn't notice. Not wanting her to be embarrassed, he ended up not saying anything but that didn't change how concerned he was with what he just witnessed.

"With happiness in his heart, Audric gave his blessing to the young couple and agreed that they had found the best match for each other. As they walked back to the castle, the news had spread already and the locals were all rejoicing that Denalla and Sir Aylwin were going to be wed. Denalla's younger brother met the two men in the courtyard and also gave his blessing on the union. Standing on the edge of the courtyard were, Denalla, her sister and her mother, all beaming from ear to ear as they had anxiously awaited to see if the elder nobleman would give his approval."

Christian looked over and gave a knowing glance to Maggie. She seemed to be feeling a little better then nodded that he should continue with his story. Placing the handkerchief back in her backpack, she had pulled a notebook out of her backpack. Occasionally he would see her writing things down in the book as he spoke but, to his surprise, she never stopped him. She nodded back as Christian reached inside of his backpack and pulled out a bottle of water. They sat in silence as the water in the loch quietly splashed against the stones on the beach. The sun was making its descent towards the top of the mountain that rose on the other side of the loch. Taking a brief recess on his story telling he opened the bottle of water and took a long drink. As he brought the bottle of water back to rest on his leg, Maggie shifted in her seat, making it clear that she was growing impatient with his delay and wanted him to continue. Placing the lid back on the bottle, he began to speak again. He was briefly interrupted by a pair of ducks that landed in the water and began quacking loudly at each other. That lasted only a few moments before they swam off looking for food. With a smile on his face, he continued.

"It was about six months after the wedding when Audric received word that the king of England was requesting that each nobleman in the north send his top five best knights to go and fight for the crown.

There was a growing war as some of the clans from the highlands of Scotland were trying to win their independence. This infuriated the king because it was showing his foreign enemies that he was at war with that, he wasn't strong enough to rule his entire land."

"Audric knew that his daughter wasn't going to be happy when she found out this news. Sir Aylwin and Denalla were newly married and had already begun their family. Denalla found out earlier that week that she was with child and like most first time parents, she was nervous about telling anyone the news. Soon she would learn that her beloved husband was going to head out to war."

"Sir Aylwin was one of the best knights that Audric had known. The young soldier had served the nobleman for a few years at that point. He was confident that his son-in-law would be fine going off to battle and would return once the war was over. However, he wasn't sure that, as strong as she was, his daughter would be just as confident. Audric, being the caring father he was, soon realized the fears of his son in law's departure, when one day the three of them were in the banquet hall."

"Sir Aylwin was in the large hall when the dispatch riders had brought the news. They knew who the best knights in the area were so there was no way he could lie and say that his son in law was dead or injured. As the two men spoke, Audric was broken hearted. He didn't want to lose his best knight but even more than that, the last thing he wanted was to see his daughter separated from the love of her life. He was at an impasse on what to do."

"The king's messengers left the castle to head on to the next stop on their list, with commitment from Audric that his men would arrive at the king's side within one week. The nobleman took his son in law to the side to discuss his options, few as they may be." Christian paused again as Maggie was now in full note taking mode. He waited until she caught up and she nodded for him to continue.

It was now late in the afternoon and Christian was looking over at Maggie. He could tell she was eager to hear the rest of the legend. "Do you want me to finish the story this evening or would you like to wait until another day?"

Maggie was getting hungry. They had lunch several hours ago but, as was usual, she wasn't in the habit of eating much so her stomach was starting to grumble. She had been drinking her diet soda while they were on the castle grounds and at first that was curbing the hunger. After this long, however, that no longer did the trick. Now she wanted something to eat. However, the story was holding her attention, so she was torn on what she wanted to do. "How about you continue on for a little while longer and then we go get dinner? Did you have plans for dinner?"

Christian agreed that he was starting to feel the bite of hunger. It had been almost four hours that they had been going over the legend. Maggie had stopped him a few times to ask him some clarifying questions. He was happy to hear her ask and quietly hoped that the information he was giving her would help with the project she was intently trying to finish so she could complete her Master's Degree. Maggie continued to write in her notebook, leaving him to sit in silence. Christian sat watching his friend finish her note taking. She had an elegant quality about her that he could never remember noticing in anyone else he had ever known. It added to the beauty of the woman now sitting with him on the banks of a loch at the base of a mountain in the beautiful country in the world.

CHAPTER SEVEN

Christian had watched as Maggie wrote in her notebook. She had been taking notes as he was talking, but continued writing after he paused to take a drink of water. He assumed that she was writing an inspiration so he kept quiet. The time passed by fast and they were just over halfway through the story of Sir Aylwin and Denalla. Now they were trying to decide if they should continue or go get dinner and continue there. It had been a pleasant afternoon as they spent the afternoon in the same place that the story Christian was telling had happened.

"Ok, I will continue for another half an hour and then we go grab some food. I am starting to get a little hungry myself." She agreed and ate a piece of chewy candy that she pulled out of her backpack.

"If you are getting tired or your hunger is getting too much, let me know and we will stop." Maggie was getting tired but she really wanted to hear the rest. They finally agreed to continue on with the story and Christian continued with the Legend of Loch Grádh.

"Audric had a quiet dinner with his wife, daughter, and son in law that evening to discuss options. It seemed like a futile effort because when it really came down to it there really was only one. Sir Aylwin had no choice and everyone sitting at the table knew that he would do his duty. The nobleman was very proud of his son in law, even though Audric knew that this quality about him would break his daughter's heart."

"The day that he left was a sad day throughout the area. Most of the people were there to watch as the horses were loaded and the knights prepared to leave their loved ones behind. Denalla's little brother was one of the men that was chosen to go with the group. Audric knew this was his older son's doing and this infuriated him even more at losing both of his sons and son in law to the greed of the ruthless king. With the exception of Denalla's little brother, the men riding with Sir Aylwin, the lead knight, had been a part of the garrison of knights for only a short time. Sir Aylwin had never been in battle with them, but if his father in law trusted them, then he would. In that very moment though, the only thing that Sir Aylwin had on his mind was that all of this was breaking his wife's heart."

"Just before he was about to mount up on his horse, Sir Aylwin walked over to his beautiful wife who was standing less than five feet away with her parents and her sisters watching the saddening scene unfold. Sir Aylwin took his father in law's hand and gave it a firm shake when the father stepped between the young couple. Audric wasn't going to settle for that and gave the young man, who had stolen his daughter's heart, a hug and told him that he was proud of him. He gave a glance to his younger son and said that same thing, but the younger man just turned his head away, waiting for the order from Sir Aylwin that they were to depart."

"Sir Aylwin went down the line of family and then finally arrived in front of his wife. He pulled her close with his arms tight around her. Her tears ran down her face as they continued to embrace. Just before he let her go, he whispered something in her ear that no one standing around was able to hear."

Christian was staring off across the water as he tried to picture the scene and the heartache that must have been felt by those standing and watching. He could imagine it because he had suffered enough heartache in his own life. It was that pain from his past that encouraged him to leave the United States and move to Scotland and it wasn't anything that he ever wanted to have to feel again.

Maggie just watched as her friend paused with what he was saying. She knew that he had his own secrets but she wasn't sure that she could ever do or say anything that would help him. So she just sat for a few moments and finished taking her notes. She took a drink of her soda and then cleared her throat when she had finished writing. The clearing of her throat brought Christian out of his thoughts.

Christian continued. "While her husband was gone fighting a war that no one really understood beyond the evil greed of the king, Denalla would go to the church to pray for the safe return of her beloved. Her faith in God was more than just ritual. She fully believed in the Heavenly God and Father of her Lord and Savior Jesus. The lovely young noblewoman knew that the only way that her Sir Aylwin would return safely was by the grace of God. If he didn't, she knew that he would be safe in His arms until they were reunited according to his plan."

Maggie watched as Christian wiped a tear that was beginning to fall out of the corner of his eye. She was impressed that he was such a strong man and that he was able to cry in front of a woman. Most men tried to be such tough guys that they were unable to even do that. Quietly he continued. "The day came when she received word that her beloved Sir Aylwin had fallen in battle. Most people would have taken that news and went into such painful mourning that they wouldn't have survived it. The legend goes that she immediately went into the church and Audric made sure that no one bothered her until she came back out. Less than two hours later, she did. There were no tears. There didn't seem to be any sorrow. A strong woman walked out and went about her new life as a widow just as she was supposed to."

"It is rumored that the strength she felt was from a story in the bible when David lost his child. Prior to the child's death David had been in mourning over the child's sickness. David was praying for healing up until the child's passing. At that point David ended the mourning and continued praising God. David knew that his child was in heaven and that there was not going to be any more pain for that young child. He had put his faith in God and no matter the outcome, he would not let his faith falter. Denalla was trying to do the same thing. So every morning, after she would eat her small breakfast and tend to her growing child, she would go off to the church with the little one in tow. She would spend a good hour in there praying and giving thanks for the child and the short time she was able to share with the man she loved more than she ever thought she could. Outside of the church door there were a few rose bushes. Every day she would pick a rose from the bush just inside the castle walls and carried it down to the water of the loch and to throw it in. The waves would take the flower and carry it off into the mist."

"Audric was impressed with the strength that his daughter showed during the time her husband off fighting and after finding out about his passing. He knew there was nothing he could do to bring him back to her but if there had been a way, he would have surely done it. One day he was talking with his daughter and his grandson near the loch." Christian paused and pointed to the spot they had just been sitting. "Right where we were just at, so the legend goes." Maggie smiled trying to picture the scene. "Audric asked his daughter what he could do to honor her husband. He turned and looked across the water and asked what the name of the loch was. Denalla didn't know as she believed they had never given the loch a name. Her loving father suggested they name it Sir Aylwin. "

"Denalla, who truly loved her husband, was not fond of it."

"Then the idea hit the nobleman. 'We will name it Loch Grádh. I have never witnessed more love between two people than I have between you and your husband. You two set such a good example. The family loves you both. The entire people in the surrounding area love you two as well. You are right, Sir Aylwin, isn't the right name, Loch Grádh is the perfect name.' "

"From that day forward this body of water and surrounding area had been named, Loch Grádh, meaning 'lake of love'. Denalla was very thankful to her father for what he had done. The legend has it that every day a rose was thrown into the loch to honor the love of the young couple. It is also said that it was to honor the love of a father to his daughter."

Christian finished the story and waited as Maggie removed a clean handkerchief from her back packet and then dried her own tears. She laid the cloth down next to her and finished writing a few notes that she had left to add to her growing notebook.

"Do you have any questions?" Christian asked waiting for her to respond with a question from the story.

"Thank you for telling me the extended version. It is definitely a heartfelt story. Before we get into questions about the legend, I do have one thing to ask."

"Please, don't hesitate."

"Can we go eat? I am so hungry.'

They both laughed and agreed that it was time to get something to eat before the grumbling of their stomachs woke up the entire countryside.

~~~~~~~~~~

Christian continued with the story as he described the bagpiper part of the story to Maggie. There wasn't much to tell on that part of the story though. What Christian did tell her, was the very little he was able to piece together from his own research at the castle and local legends about the mysterious bagpiper. Maggie was gathering her things and packing them back in to her backpack as he told he this brief piece of the story.

The original bagpiper lived in the castle with the

nobleman and his family. He was conscripted to play as Denalla went to the loch each day to throw the rose into the water. Some believed that the bagpiper that Maggie and Christian heard when they arrived at the castle that day was the ghost of this man. Christian, however, did not believe in ghost stories so he shrugged that idea off and just enjoyed the thought of listening to the music whenever he heard it.

There was even less information about the mysterious bagpiper that supposedly still played in the area. Even though people claimed to faintly hear the music, no one had actually ever seen the piper in person, making the legend even more mysterious.

"How much of this story is true?" she asked him as they headed back to his car.

"Legends, I have found, are based on truth." Christian smiled. "Only the evidence can prove it one way or another."

CHAPTER EIGHT

For the next week Maggie had been working on her thesis. Christian hadn't seen her and barely talked to her. She had been so busy with the plethora of information that he had given her, she want to make sure she didn't forget any of it.

Christian had a slow day at the Royal Infirmary and when his supervisor asked if anyone would like to leave early, Christian jumped at the chance. He had come up with what he thought was a good idea on his way into work. It had put a smile on his face for the whole day. He was in a great mood as he left the building where he spent a lot of his days when he wasn't at the castle. He crossed the parking lot and headed to his car. Once inside, he removed his cell from the side pocket of his navy blue cargo pant scrubs. He dialed his closest friend and by the time he had hung up with her, he was in an even better mood. Christian had been through the ringer and back in his life. He did his best to maintain a positive attitude and most of the people in his life would say that he did. It would however, be a rare statement that he was ever described as an overly happy person. The scars of his life ran too deep for that to be a true statement. Today was a different story. Today he was happy. Today he was going to spend the afternoon with his dear friend Margaret Elizabeth Greene.

~~~~~~~~~~~

It was just after nine in the morning on Tuesday when her phone rang. Maggie was sitting in the living room of the cottage when she heard the ring coming from the counter in the kitchen where it was charging. Maggie didn't know what to expect because her phone rarely rang when she wasn't expecting a call. She had a weekly conversation with her parents but that wasn't until Sunday. Neither of them had any doctor's appointments that week, which would have been why they would have spoken earlier than Sunday, so it couldn't have been them. Due to her sister's busy schedule, she hadn't spoken to her since she first arrived in Scotland. She didn't need to check in with her professor about her thesis for two more weeks. That was the list of the people she thought could be calling her at that moment. She started to get a little anxious as she made her way across the worn wooden floor of the hallway leading from the living room to the kitchen.

Maggie's stomach rumbled and she felt like she wanted

to throw up the very little breakfast she had eaten a few hours earlier. She had lost some weight in the short time that she had been there and she knew it had to do with her inability to not worry and always think the worst thing was going to happen to her. When she picked up the cell phone, she smiled as her heart leapt. It was Christian, unexpectedly. A moment of fear started to creep into her mind in the brief moment before she lifted the phone up to her ear. All the times they had spent together had been at Stewart Castle or at The Pipers as he had been helping her with her research. Their meetings so far had always been planned before they left whatever they were doing at the time. Maggie really preferred to have things scheduled in advance so she knew what to expect. This call, however, broke the unwritten but seemingly understood rule and to her surprise, it didn't make her feel anxious anymore. On the contrary, it made her very happy and excited to hear from him.

"Hi Christian," Maggie said, even before the phone was all the way up to her ear. She wasn't able to contain her excitement.

"Hi Maggie, how is your day going?" Christian was trying to hide his own excitement.

"Good, thank you for asking." She paused then added, "aren't you supposed to be at work?" She was still happy but beginning to wonder why he called on a day they weren't planning on seeing each other. Then her heart stopped for a brief moment, but not in a good way. She started thinking the worst that either something happened to him at work or he was calling to cancel the day they had planned to get together in two days.

"Well I was but we were slow so I volunteered to leave early." He was smiling, waiting for response to his statement.

Maggie was smiling as well, not that he could see her, even though inside she was thinking the worst. He was ok so nothing happened at work. So in her eyes, there could only be one other reason why he called. She braced herself for the hurtful blow that was about to be delivered.

To her surprise, he didn't say what she expected. In fact what he did say kind of shocked her.

"So," Christian said, "I am going to stop by on my way home and pick you up. We will go and spend the day together."

She was shocked but a little happy that he was being so forward. This wasn't his normal character but instead of being put off by it so much, it impressed her. "What do you have in mind?" Maggie asked the question but in truth she didn't really care about the answer. She really didn't want to spend the day around the cottage and was happy that on Christian's unexpected day off from work, she was his first thought.

"Nothing at all," was his only reply

As strange as his answer was to her, Maggie surprised herself by being okay with it. "That sounds interesting."

"The only thing that I will say is be ready in 20 minutes and I hope you are hungry."

With that he hung up the phone, leaving Maggie to stand in the kitchen for a few minutes trying to figure out what she should wear. Knowing that no matter what she decided on, Christian would genuinely compliment her on it. She made herself set her phone down and head to the bedroom to get dressed. Digging through her belongings she found a tan and red plaid skirt that came down about half way between her knees and ankles. It was stylish and she thought it would keep her warm. She added a black turtle neck cable knit sweater to her ensemble. After fixing her hair, she finished off her outfit with a pair of knee high leather boots that zipped on the side.

As was typical of Christian he arrived a few minutes early. He had changed out of his scrubs and into a pair of cargo shorts, a polo shirt, and a zip up fleece jacket with a pair of slip on gym shoes. He looked very relaxed and happy and that put Maggie in even higher spirits. They made small talk as she gathered up her things to get ready to walk out the door. As he was holding the door open, Maggie paused and went back into the kitchen to grab a diet soda out of the refrigerator. He knew what she was going to get and for a brief moment, his smiled faltered. He had hoped that she would be able to enjoy the day without her extra soda mix but he was determined to give her such a great day that she wouldn't even think about that bottle.

As she tucked the bottle of soda into her purse, Maggie turned to Christian, smiled and said, "Are you ready to go?"

He forced his smile to returned, as he held the door open for her again and they both headed to the car. Maggie was surprised to see a picnic basket sitting in the backseat of his car. She wanted to know what was inside and what he had planned but decided to not give it any more thought and sat back in the seat and enjoyed the ride as he drove down her street and out onto the road that led out to the countryside.

~~~~~~~~~~

Christian had been looking at a map a couple of weeks earlier while working at the castle. It had been a slow day and he had been there most of the day by himself. One of the places he thought he would like to visit was Dunbar. He had heard some of the stories of the coastal town and thought it would be nice to visit. On his way into the hospital that bright spring morning, he decided that he would take Maggie to see it. Now, as they were getting into his car in front of her cozy country side cottage, he asked over the top of the car if she had any suggestions on what they should do on their unexpected day together. A bit of a silly question, being that he had already planned the day.

"I'm fine with whatever you come up with. I am sure no matter what we do, we will have a great day together." She said as they were driving out for their day together.

Christian smiled and nodded in agreement. Maggie trusted him, he could tell and he never wanted to do anything to break that trust. He headed out to the country road leading to the east and Maggie rolled down her window and asked him if wouldn't mind rolling down the rest of them to let in the breeze from the drive. It was a nice day with only a slight chill in the air.

By the time they arrived in Dunbar, Maggie Green was the most relaxed she had been since arriving in Scotland. They talked very little on the drive from Loch Grádh to Dunbar. Christian was enjoying watching the scenery go by and Maggie was drifting in and out of sleep. He was happy to see her resting, knowing that she really needed to let go of some of the stress that she held onto. He didn't know much about her past but he was putting things together the more time they spent with each other.

Christian's experience as a nurse taught him to listen for the things that were not said and to watch the body language of the person he was talking to. He had been a nurse for so long, that it was so instinctual that he did it without even thinking about it. He knew she had an eating disorder, and from the few times they had gone to get something to eat, he was guessing it was bulimia. He also knew there was a drinking issue. He knew these things but he was waiting for her to bring them up.

It wasn't a long drive but it had done for Maggie exactly what Christian had hoped. She hadn't had a drink from her bottle of diet soda mixed with whatever type of alcohol she put in with it. He wanted to change his way of thinking at the moment because he didn't want to be stressed over the alcohol issue. They took this day trip as a way to get away from this stresses of life for both of them. They were pulled into a parking space next to a restaurant called The Highlands that was on the southern side of the town of Dunbar. She stirred and turned to her right to look at him as he put the car in park. They sat there for a moment discussing what they wanted to do first. To his surprise, Maggie asked if it was ok if they grabbed a bit to eat before they did some sightseeing. She was implying that she wanted to see what was in the picnic basket in the back seat but Christian had another idea.

"Sure, let's try this place. I've heard they have great shepherd's pie." He had found this place online and was looking forward to his favorite dish.

"Ok, sounds good." Maggie was caught a little off guard but since he was a man full of surprises, she figured he had something else in mind. She gathered herself together and fluffed her long blond hair before they got out of the car. They both stretched the drive out of their muscles and then headed into the restaurant for a good lunch.

CHAPTER NINE

"I'm surprised we are here. I thought you had made a lunch for us." She said as they were eating the delicious meals that were in front of them.

Christian was dipping a piece of fresh bread in the gravy of his shepherd's pie. "I am not sure what you mean?"

Maggie was enjoying her piece of baked fish with a side of rice. "I noticed the picnic basket in the back seat. I figured you had made us lunch and that we were going to go to a park somewhere."

Christian smiled. "I figured you would think that. I did that to keep up the surprise."

"What is that supposed to mean?" She was noticeably getting a little frustrated.

"I was tasked with cleaning out one of the storage closets at the castle. I came across that basket and asked Iain what they were going to do with it and the other things they were cleaning out. He told me that if I could find any of it a good home, it was mine to take." He paused as he watched her expression soften back into a smile. "I thought you might like it, especially since it was something used by your family over 90 years ago."

Maggie was caught off guard again. It was the second time in a matter of 2 ½ hours that he had surprised her and left her speechless.

Christian didn't do the things he did for any self recognition. He did them for Maggie because he wanted to see her smile. When she looked over at him, she did smile and it made him happy to see that she was enjoying herself. He didn't believe it was up to others to make him happy but her happiness made his heart lighter.

She was beginning to learn that this man was full of surprises and the more she spent time with him, the more she wanted to spend time with him. This day had only just begun and she was having the best day she had in a long time. She was relaxed and was sitting in a coastal town in Scotland enjoying a good lunch with great company. What more could she ask for?

~~~~~~~~~~~

They were only going to be spending one day in Dunbar so they made a plan for the few things they would be able to get in on such short time. The things they decided on would end up giving them both memories that would last a life time. Both Maggie and Christian knew that it really wasn't the places they would visit that would give them the wonderful memories but it was the company. They both had enjoyed each other's company since the first day they met. Neither of them had been looking for someone to enter their lives and neither had expected the other to make such an impact. Christian was happy to have Maggie in his life. He couldn't get her out of his mind. While they were sitting in the little restaurant in Dunbar, he was watching her and how excited she was for the day ahead. What made Christian even happier was that Maggie had left her bottle of diet cola in the car. He wanted to show her that she didn't need that in order to have a good day. He wasn't going to say anything to her about it, but hopefully she would just pick up on the hint.

"Are you ready to go," he asked as they had finished eating and the bill was paid.

"Yes I am, I just need to go to the restroom before we leave. I need to brush my teeth." And with that, she was up from the table and walking to the ladies room.

Christian's heart sank a bit because he knew what was going on. She was a beautiful woman. She had a heart of gold. He had no idea what she saw when she looked in the mirror, but it was obviously not the same thing that he did. That thought broke his heart a little more. He knew a lot of people that struggled with self worth. He had his struggles as well. Christian had heard a sermon once and the pastor spoke a true statement that had stuck with him for all these years. The pastor has said, "Everyone has their faults and skeletons in their closet. Whatever they are, we can only be genuine caring people when we love others the way we want to beloved. That means that we have to look beyond the faults and love the person underneath the pain."

Those words meant the world to Christian. He knew the

pastor was right and that was exactly how Jesus loves. The young man tried to put those words into his everyday life, including his job. He knew it helped him to be compassionate with people that in the past would have driven him nuts. He knew that being that way brought him closer to Jesus. Those words also helped him with the things that Maggie seemed to be going through. He knew she wouldn't open up to him about those issues but he figured he would just continue to be caring and understanding and be the friend that she needed. Besides, he really enjoyed her company.

~~~~~~~~~~

Dunbar castle was no exception to the amazing castles that she had visited since being there. This castle was located on a little island of its own just off the eastern coast in the North Sea. It was a good location to make it difficult for warring forces to attack it. There were three stone bridges that connected the island to the mainland. This isolation was good for its protection which made Dunbar a nice place for people to settle.

As they walked around the castles ground, Maggie and Christian tried to imagine what life would have been like over five hundred years ago. Christian marveled at how deep Maggie was thinking about the area they walked. She would ask questions, like where he thought the marketplace was located, how many people he thought lived in the area, and so on. In the grand scheme of things, the questions didn't really mean anything. It was just Maggie getting absorbed in the moment. That was something that Christian always had a difficult time doing. He was always thinking about the next thing he needed to do. He wasn't able to just live in the moment. Watching Maggie made him even more impressed with her.

The two of them walked around the grounds for over three hours, just talking and looking at everything around them. Maggie would stop and look at the stone that made up the walls of the main building. She knelt down and ran her fingers over the green grass growing in the yard between the walls. Most of the time, Christian just watched her. It made him think of one of the Bible stories that he had enjoyed as a young boy. It went something like, "...unless you are converted and become as little children, you will by no means enter the kingdom of heaven." It took Christian a long time to understand what that meant. One day it finally hit him. It was about approaching the Lord with awe struck amazement. That is how Maggie approached most of her life. She took great pleasure in the small things and wanted to know as much as she could to understand all that was around her. Christian admired her for this.

Neither of them realized just how long they had been walking until the horn blew to let them know it was closing time. They decided to head back to town to take a look around before they had to head back to Loch Grádh.

Maggie and Christian were walking up and down the streets turning their heads to look at things in shop windows that may have grabbed their attention. Since they weren't really shopping for anything in particular, they just kept walking at a very casual pace. Christian and Maggie were both enjoying each other's company and both of them knew that after that day, their relationship would not be the same. They were no longer just two casual friends that met just to work on a thesis. Their friendship was moving at a pace they were comfortable with and to a place they both welcomed.

~~~~~~~~~~

They made it back to Loch Grádh Just after nine that evening. Maggie had fallen asleep on the way back and Christian drove in silence replaying the entire day in his head. He was so impressed with how the day turned out. Maggie was usually so reserved but today was different. As he occasionally looked over at her leaning against the passenger window, asleep and hopefully dreaming of something relaxing, he was happy to see a peace about her. He believed the day had helped to calm whatever demons would tear their claws at her. The one thought he had that made his mind quiet the rest of the trip back, was that she didn't take the bottle of diet soda mix with her the entire time they were out walking around. A smile crawled across his face and stayed there until he pulled up in front of her cottage to drop her off.

CHAPTER TEN

Christian was enjoying a quiet night sitting at The Pipers. It had been two days since his trip to Dunbar with Maggie. She had spent the last two days working hard on her thesis while Christian enjoyed a few quiet days off from work. Christian wasn't one to drink alcohol which made his frequent time sitting at the pub a bit strange but he did it just because he enjoyed watching the people and getting to know his neighbors.

"How are you doing Lad?" Angus said as he came over to refill his soda.

"I'm doing just great." Christian knew that Angus was trying to get at something because he would rarely walk over and strike up a conversation with him. Christian never took offense to it. It was just the bar keepers way. Today, he was going to make him talk more.

"How was your trip to the east coast with the lovely American lass?"

Christian was about to answer but Angus added to his comment.

"When are you two stubborn Americans actually going to tell each other how you feel? Everyone in the pub can see it, why can't the two of you?" A little frustrated with this American man he walked away mumbling something in ancient Gaelic and walked back to the kitchen to bring out some food for another patron.

Christian had thought that very same question a few times and in truth, had never found an answer. Sure, he had his excuses that he would try to convince himself of but in the end, they were only that, excuses. The truth was that he was afraid to let anyone in again. He would say when asked why he was alone, that it would take a lifetime to put the dust of his heart together just to make them broken pieces. Then the broken pieces needed to be put together to make it whole. His past did a great job of destroying his heart and hope. Now all he wanted to do was serve Jesus by being a compassionate nurse and friend to anyone He brought into his life.

As he spent time with Maggie though, he began to think that maybe he wasn't as afraid as he first thought he open his heart.

Maybe, just maybe, his heart could feel again.

Maybe, there was a chance for him to love again.

~~~~~~~~~~~

"Why don't you ever talk about yourself?" They were sitting in the cafeteria of the Infirmary eating lunch while he was on his break. Maggie had called late last night and asked if it would be okay if she brought him a home cooked lunch the next day. It was a very pleasant surprise for him so he told her that it would be a great idea. He told her when he usually took his lunch and they agreed she would be in the cafeteria by the time he was able to get away. What Maggie didn't tell him was that she was going to be at the hospital because she had a doctor's appointment. Maggie had woken up feeling horrible the day before. The urgency of the appointment was that she had coughed up a little bit of blood again. It might end up being nothing, but she figured it would be better to be safe than sorry.

The two of them had been spending a lot of time together recently and were really getting along better than either of them had expected. Maggie knew that Christian was in medicine but didn't want to share with him what was going on until she knew for sure what it was. She didn't want to worry this kind man.

The time they did spend together had been a joy to each of them. Maggie had opened up and shared with him more than she ever thought she could have imagined that she would have. Maggie had a good heart that she kept well protected. Christian did the same thing with his heart. He kept his heart hidden to avoid any more pain from seeping in but also from any of his skeletons getting out. He had changed a lot over the years and he believed it was for the good. If any of those secrets of his past were to ever escape, he felt that it would ruin him.

"To be honest, I really enjoy learning more about you. It makes my day to listen to you." It was an honest statement, just not a complete statement.

"That's nice, but I really want to get to know you," she said softly. She was touched by his compliment but hurt by the distance that he put between his heart and others.

"Maggie, I am truly sorry. I wasn't trying to be evasive." Now that wasn't an honest statement. He knew it. As much as he was trying to avoid pain from opening his heart, he ended up hurting his friend. He tried to offer an explanation but, in the end, he wasn't sure if it mattered to her. "I've spent my entire life by myself hiding my heart and being told that I was worthless. I figured if you were able to see what I keep behind the wall, you would think and feel the same way. The last thing I want is for you to think that of me. Besides, your life is so much more interesting and intriguing to listen to."

She was trying to hold back a few tears as she battled conflicting emotions that she was going through. "Anyone can say that about themselves. The truth is, that is a copout answer."

Christian was caught off guard by the strength in her voice. It was the same strength in her that made her able to travel to not only a different country but a different continent by herself to work on her thesis paper. It was that same strength that just rebuked him for, in essence, being a coward and being selfish, for not opening up to her the way she had with him.

"Hey Christian, is this your American friend we have heard so much about?" Payton Nicole said as she walked past on her way to get her lunch from the cafeteria line.

"Hi Payton, yes this is Maggie. Maggie this is Payton." Maggie turned to shake her hand. "Payton and I work in the ER together," thankful for the interruption.

Maggie smiled, "It is very nice to meet you." She was back to her normal cheerful self. There wasn't one hint of the sadness she was feeling just moments before. She wasn't being fake when she was talking to him and she wasn't being fake when she was introduced to his coworker.

"How are you enjoying our country so far?" asked the friendly blond nurse.

Maggie seemed to relax even more as the two ladies chatted for a few minutes. This gave Christian a quick opportunity to eat the egg salad sandwich that Maggie had waiting for him when he went on break. She had made this at home and brought that for him with a bottle of soda and a bag of pita chips. They chatted for a few minutes, and then Payton Nicole excused herself from them and walked over to the food line to get her lunch.

After she was out of ear shot, Maggie turned to Christian and waited for him to say something. He really didn't need the prompting and apologized again for the way he had been acting lately. Maggie was happy that he wanted to get to know her, but she really wanted him to open up as well. "Maggie, you are a dear sweet friend. It was never my intent to hurt you."

She knew he was being sincere. There was nothing about him that she thought was malicious. "I understand. I am usually the same way. With you though, I didn't want to push you away by being closed off. I thought you would do the same thing."

"I am really enjoying our time together and I do respect what you are saying. I will be better at that." He was being very sincere. Christian did care about her and knew that he was in the wrong. "In the meantime, I do have to go back to work but we can hang out in the next day or so and I will tell you anything you want to know."

"That would be great," she replied, clearly even more relaxed now than when he had first met up with her for lunch. "Will you call me later?"

"I would love to. I should be home around 8:30 this evening, will that be too late?" He asked as he was standing up getting ready to head back to his department.

"That would be fine. When you call, I will tell you about my doctor's appointment that I just came from."

"Ok," he said, a little caught off guard, "and remind me to tell you what Angus said to me yesterday."

CHAPTER ELEVEN

Christian spent the rest of the afternoon at work trying not to focus on what could have possibly happened at her appointment. Maggie had been more interested in getting him to open up to her than she was to tell him what had happened at her appointment. Fortunately, it was a steady afternoon at the Infirmary and the rest of his shift went by fast. He didn't have much time to focus on anything else. It went by before Christian even knew what time it was.

The evening shift came in and patient report was given. Christian was able to leave a little earlier than normal and was happy to be making his way home. He was happy to have the next day off and was planning to just sit around his flat and relax. There were things he needed to catch up on.

He had been spending so much time with Maggie that some of the things that he needed to do were getting pushed to the side. He didn't regret it but they were things that needed some attention. Christian knew that he had continuing education that needed to be done. It was a requirement in order to keep the licensing for his RN. Even though Christian didn't have any plans to return to his home town in northwest Ohio, he kept up with licensing requirements there as well. When his coworkers asked him why, if he enjoyed Scotland as much as he did, would he waste the time and money. His only answer was, 'just in case'. So he was planning on spending the next day doing just that.

~~~~~~~~~~

He finally made it home after work and was settling into his own routine, take off his scrubs, take a quick shower and then a light dinner. He wanted to go for a walk since the rain that had been falling all day had finally stopped on his way home. When Christian was planning on traveling to Scotland for work, a lot of people told him that he was crazy because of all the rain. Since he first arrived, he never minded the rain. It wasn't 'rain' like what he was used to back from where he came. There when it rained there were many variations of it. It could be a torrential down pour. It could be a heavy rain where the drops pelted the skin. Other times it was just a soft rain that fell like it was misting the ground to give it a nice watering. Since his time in Scotland, that was the type of rain he experienced the most. At times, it could be tiresome, but it was never anything that made him run from one point to another so he wouldn't get soaked.

That night, even though it had been raining, Christian

wanted to get out and get some fresh air. He had been cooped up inside the Infirmary all day and just needed time outside. He also figured that while he was out, he would put on his headphones that connected to his cell phone and call Maggie.

When he stepped out of his flat and out onto the sidewalk, he stopped, closed his eyes and took a deep breath of the fresh air. It instantly put him into a better mood. He turned and started walking towards the end of town. There was a bench at the end of the main street that he would occasionally sit on to watch the setting sun. Today he remembered to bring his camera. He was an amateur photographer and enjoyed taking pictures of his surroundings. When he looked back at the pictures that he took, he would always thank God for the beauty that He made for our enjoyment.

Christian walked at a good pace and made it to the bench before the sun started its final descent below the horizon. Even though the rain had stopped earlier, the clouds only had time to partially clear. The color in the sky as the sun was setting was one of the most spectacular sights that Christian had ever seen. The pink, red and purple hue to the clouds and the sky made Christian offer a prayer of thanksgiving to God as he sat and watched and took pictures of what he was seeing. There were times that he would pray a lengthy prayer and other times a shorter prayer. In that moment, all he could say was, "Heavenly Father, thank you for the beauty that you have shown me this night. May you always remind me that You are there, In Jesus name I pray, Amen."

After he finished his prayer, Christian dialed Maggie's phone. He was still snapping a few pictures on his camera when she answered. Christian knew that his prayer put him in the right frame of heart to be able to handle whatever it was that Maggie was about to say about her doctor's appointment earlier that day.

"Let me guess," she said when she answered the phone, "you are taking pictures of the beautiful sunset." It really wasn't a question as much as it was a statement that she did know him fairly well.

"I just couldn't help it. It was a tough day at work and I just needed to get out and get some fresh air. The sunset was just an added bonus from Jesus."

Christian normally didn't mention anything about his job. Maggie knew that it had a lot to do with how he was trained back in the U.S where HIPAA was practiced very closely. Healthcare workers back in the states were required by law to never discuss patient information with anyone. Christian held to that practice when he arrived at the Infirmary. He was very strict on never discussing anything about work, so she was surprised to hear him mention it. Maggie was even more surprised with what he said next.

"Today was a tough day, not because of anything that happened with patients in the ER. It was a tough day because I haven't been able to get out of my head what could've happened at your appointment."

Maggie was speechless for a moment. She was continually surprised at just how much he cared for her. They had not crossed the line into a romantic relationship yet, but she could tell that her friend really did care.

"That is very sweet of you to say that. I didn't mean to keep you in suspense all afternoon." She went on to explain that she was going to need an endoscopy to figure out why she had started bleeding when she was coughing while they were at the castle a couple weeks prior. Even though he already knew it, Maggie finally admitted to him that this had occurred more times than the first time he noticed it. She knew he was concerned but he was very respectful of her to not bring it up. She went on to explain that they did some blood work and found that everything seemed to be ok with the exception of her liver enzymes being slightly elevated. At that time, those didn't concern the doctor too much.

Christian knew that Maggie was putting something into the diet soda that she carried with her. The little bit of information she just admitted to, led him to believe that there was more going on than a little blood on a cloth when she coughed. He knew that she would end up needing more than just an endoscopy. As she continued to tell him the minor details, he quietly prayed that Jesus would watch over her.

They ended the call stating that they would get together the next day, about the same time, to watch the setting sun. Maggie wanted to work on her paper and Christian had told her that he had things to do as well. Maggie asked if he would be willing to take a few pictures of her so she could send them to her parents. Christian said that he would when they met the next evening.

Once they were off the phone, Christian sat and watched as the sun finally dropped below the horizon. He sat for a little while longer thinking about everything that was going on with Maggie. He didn't want there to be anything seriously wrong with her. He was growing more and more fond of her and he couldn't bear the thought of her in pain. However his instinct and experience were telling him that there was just cause to be concerned. Christian knew what the doctors were looking for. "Lord please help her with her health and struggles," he said out loud as his heart was breaking. This emotional up and down that he was on was something new to him. He knew trying to open his heart to love her, but it seemed the more he did, the more his heart was breaking.

He was starting to get very cold by the time he slowly made his way back to his flat. It was normally a 20 minute walk, but that night it took him over 45 min to walk back. He was in no hurry and just wanted to enjoy the evening outside. He was trying to find peace, the same peace he had prior to finding out what happened at Maggie's appointment.

CHAPTER TWELVE

From the moment she breezed into his life, they had spent as much time as they could together. She had her days where she was glued to her computer typing away on her thesis. She was trying to get this accomplished so she could spend more time exploring the area and as much of Scotland as she could before she went back to the United States. She was fascinated with this country and the more she learned, the more she wanted to learn. As she was making progress on her paper, she began to feel like the whole 'thesis paper writing' exercise of higher education was trivial. Real life was not in that paper. Real life was all around her, out in the grove on the eastern side of the loch that she was now sitting, enjoying the company of Christian and the wildlife that went about their business not paying any attention to the two watching them.

It was almost two weeks after she had been to the doctor. Christian watched for any signs of her worsening condition. Fortunately there were none. They sat near the banks of Loch Grádh finishing the picnic lunch she had made them. Maggie was acting like she wanted to ask Christian a question.

"Is there something on your mind," he asked her playfully.

"Well kind of," she replied as if she was trying to find the words to say. "I have a question about the wedding?"

"The wedding," Christian was surprised at the question and that she was asking it now. His surprise was that she hadn't asked him before that. They just enjoyed a very nice picnic at the castle. For someone who struggled with an eating disorder like she did, they did spend a lot of their time together at a meal of some sort or another. Even though the meal may have been the catalyst, he knew it was more the fellowship of them being together that was really the center point. They always had great conversation when they did talk, so it really never mattered to Christian where they met.

"Yes, when you told me the legend, you never said anything about the wedding. I'll bet it was a grand event." Maggie was beaming as she said this, trying to picture what it must have been like.

"I can see why you would think that, but that isn't the case." Christian watched her expression but to his surprise she didn't react at all. She patiently waited for him to continue.

Christian took a sip of his water and really wished he had some soda to drink. Just as he was about to ask Maggie if there was anything in the basket, she reached in and pulled out exactly what he was about to ask for. He opened the can and took a big drink. That seemed to satisfy his craving and he continued.

"The wedding was a mild affair compared to what one would find at a royal affair. Audric had tables set up in the courtyard of the castle grounds. Most of the people from the surrounding area were there. There was a lot of food served, roast turkey and roast chicken, fresh baked bread, baked pies, and seasonal fruits. It was all the things that made the celebration a feast. The people in the area were happy to contribute what they could. If you remember from what I told you about the legend, Audric was well liked as was Sir Aylwin and Denalla. All the people wanted to join in the celebration."

Maggie was listening and trying to picture what the scene must have looked like. "So far it is sounding like a grand event in the area."

"It does seem that way but that is about where all the 'grandness' seemed to end, according to legend that is." Christian went on to explain the historical wedding of the day. He explained that weddings typically had a lot of music, dancing, and there would be games.

Maggie was intrigued by this because the weddings that she had been to in her life were almost like that even now.

"However, with Sir Aylwin and Denalla's wedding, it was just about the feast and fellowship of the people. Unlike the greedy king that ruled by threats and fear, Audric was a nobleman that respected the people under his rule. He showed that by having a small wedding for his older daughter and not making the people give more than they could. He knew the king bled them dry of what they worked so hard for. Audric would never be that way."

She understood why the wedding wasn't that grand event she thought it would be for a daughter that was loved by her father as much as Denalla was. It was actually out of love for her and for the people that he ruled over that it wasn't. It showed more than respect. That act showed love in a way that she couldn't ever remember seeing before.

"There was a little music that was played. Legend has it that there were two fiddle players, a flute player and a bagpiper and that the ceremony was beautiful. There was never a doubt how much the two of them loved each other. The ceremony itself was very sweet. The priest recited some of the best verses out of the bible that described love. When the ceremony was over, the gathered crowd enjoyed a feast that was more grand than any they had ever had in that land. Unfortunately it turned out to be the last one they had on that scale."

When he was done explaining everything that had happened at the wedding, Maggie just sat staring off across the rippling water of the loch. There had been something else that she had been struggling with and at this point felt like it was time that she tried to explain to Christian how she was feeling about her paper. He sat quietly because now it was her turn to talk. The times of her opening up to him were becoming more frequent. He didn't want to ruin any momentum she had with any comments of his own. He thought the more she opened up, the more she would heal from the pain she kept locked up in her heart.

"Life is all around me. I have missed so much of life by being afraid. I have been afraid to live.' She paused briefly, collecting her thoughts. "I have even been afraid to love." Her eyes were starting to well up with tears. She turned her face away from Christian, not wanting him to see just how much this subject was affecting her. She thought about changing the subject but sat silently as she contemplated what exactly she wanted to say. He had been very kind to her. He never pressed her to talk. When she did, he never judged her. From the first day they met, he accepted her for who she was.

Her gaze led her to look out across the water to the middle of the loch. From the corner of her eye, she noticed a hawk swoop down from his circling high above. She watched the bird of prey soared just above the surface of the water. In one quick movement, the bird stretched out its legs and grabbed a fish that had been swimming just below the surface. The icy cold water rippled briefly from the hawk as he grabbed his lunch. The sun hid behind the increasing clouds that cool summer day. A breeze picked up and danced through the up stretched arms of the trees. In the silence of their conversation, they could hear the creaking of the trees not far from where they were sitting.

"Pain and hurt have a way of distorting everything around us. Distorting things so even something as good as love appears as nothing but pain." She was making no effort to hide her tears now. She had crossed the line and wanted nothing more than to let this kind man in, in behind the wall she kept up to protect herself, to protect her fragile heart. Maggie had told a lot about herself over the months and had even rebuked him for not sharing more. He responded kindly by opening up to her more and more.

He gently placed his hand on her shoulder. He felt her shuddering ever so slightly. It wasn't just the surprise of his touch but from the tears as well. His heart was breaking watching her suffer. He had learned early on that this woman was as genuine as they come. Christian believed that God gives all His children gifts that help them to serve others and bring honor to Him. He believed his gift was to read people. This served him well in his job at the hospital. It also helped when he was with his friends, the few he had. They were able to share things with him because of it. Maggie must have felt comfortable with him early on also, because from the very first meeting, she never showed an ounce of nervousness.

Christian wanted to hold her and comfort her but he felt like he would be taking advantage of her in her fragile state. He wanted to take away all the pain that she had buried in her heart but made no move other than his hand on her shoulder. He loved her very much and wanted nothing more than to hold her, help her, in any way he could. In the end he said a quiet prayer to Jesus as she calmed herself down. They sat in silence for some time as she opened her notebook and worked on her paper. Christian leaned back on the ground and watched as the clouds cleared overhead. It was now almost a completely cloudless day and he was just staring into the blueness of the sky. It didn't seem like that long before Maggie was shaking his shoulder waking him up for them to get ready to leave.

"How long was I asleep?" He asked as they gathered up the blanket and left over picnic supplies. Then he remembered, "You were crying. I am so sorry for falling asleep."

"You weren't asleep that long. I was going to wake you up, but decided to let you sleep. You seem exhausted lately." In truth, she didn't want to talk about the subject any longer and was happy to let the conversation end when it did. She knew he wouldn't let it go and that they would talk again.

"I have been. Thank you. For some reason I haven't been sleeping well the last couple of weeks." As soon as the words were out, he regretted saying them.

"It is all my fault, for telling you what happened at the doctor's visit." There was a saddened look on her face as she turned away from him.

"Actually Maggie it was something that happened at work. We had an issue with a patient and I have been wondering how everything turned out with that person." It was a sincere statement. He didn't want her stressing out thinking that he was losing sleep over her issue. Strange though as that may be, it would cause Maggie sleepless nights if she thought her friend was losing sleep over her.

"I know you can't tell me anything about it, but I will say a prayer that the patient will be ok."

"Thank you. I know that will be very helpful." That was the first time she had said anything about her faith. It put a smile on his face that lasted all the way to their cars, as they loaded everything into their respective vehicles and prepared for the short drive back to their homes.

~~~~~~~~~~

Before they drove off, Christian reminded her that they would be meeting for coffee early in the morning on Friday for their weekend trip to Aberdeen. They were both looking forward to spending some time away from the town they were both presently calling home.

It was late in the afternoon as Margaret Elizabeth Greene headed home from her long day working on her research project with Christian at the castle. She was exhausted and couldn't wait to get home and make herself a warm cup of tea. She was planning on drinking the warm drink as she was taking a hot bath and let the stress of the day, of the past couple of weeks melt away.

Maggie said that she would be ready and that she was looking forward to the time away from having to work on her paper. Fortunately it was almost done and wouldn't have to work on it much longer, other than editing it.

By the time she made it back to her cottage, she was more than ready for her cup of tea and a hot bath. She had been struggling as of late and the one thing she wanted more than anything was to soak and forget all about her issues and the paper that was taking more time than she had thought it would. The water for the tea was boiling as the tub was about half way filled. Maggie added a sugar cube and a slice of lemon to her tea and walked to the bathroom to enjoy her soak.

CHAPTER THIRTEEN

Maggie was very excited when she and Christian met for coffee before their trip. They were planning on spending the weekend together and until two days ago they had no idea where they were going to go. Maggie hadn't had a lot of time to see much of the eastern coast of Scotland. So on Thursday, they decided that they were going to take the train to Aberdeen and hike part of the coast on the North Sea. There were many things to see and he knew that the Aberdeen coast would be a lot different than the coast in Dunbar, where they had spent the day a few months back.

However, as they were drinking their warm drinks and waiting for the train, Christian realized it wasn't just the trip that she was excited about. There was something else was on her mind and Christian didn't hesitate to ask what it was. She danced around the answer as she decided to discuss things like where they would eat lunch once they arrived in Aberdeen, what other towns they would visit, etc, He soon realized that he wasn't going to get a straight answer so he let the fatigue that had been plaguing him over the last two weeks, start to win.

When Maggie looked over at him, she noticed his eyes were beginning to look a little heavy. Actually it was the dark circles under his eyes that betrayed him. It was evident that he wasn't getting much sleep. Christian had told her that work had been tough lately with some tough cases with a few of the patients. Maggie knew that although that may be a true statement, he was using that as an excuse. She knew that part of the issue was his past that was haunting him and keeping him awake by not letting his mind shut off long enough to get any rest. None of that, however, was going to put a damper on their plans for the weekend. She was getting to know him well and knew that he would do what he could so that they would enjoy their two and a half days together.

There were a lot of people that were milling about waiting for the newly arrived train to be ready for the passengers to board. There was a child that ran around where Christian and Maggie were sitting. Christian watched as the little boy was playing tag with his older sister. They were giggling and their parents were trying to quiet them down so they wouldn't bother the rest of the waiting passengers.

The train was finally ready for passengers to board so Maggie stood up and gathered her things. Not wanting his exhaustion to discourage the fun weekend they had planned, she focused on her excitement. She had been having a few rough days as of late herself. They both needed this weekend to help them relax. Maggie had had another doctor appointment and it wasn't the good news that she had hoped. She hadn't mentioned the second appointment when they were at the castle. Maggie hadn't wanted to worry her friend any more than he already was. However, now wasn't the time to focus on that. There was too much good that was in store for the next few days, so she kept the conversation light. They boarded the train and took their seats. As they became settled on the train, she couldn't contain her excitement any longer and told him why she was so excited. She began explaining to Christian about the conversation that she had with her parents earlier that morning.

"I spoke with mom and dad this morning." She was having a difficult time sitting still as the train was pulling away from the station. Watching her get this excited gave Christian a second wind and he sat up in his seat as Maggie was shifting in her chair. She was about to continue when the conductor announced that he would be checking tickets once the train left the station. She was being as patient as she could but the longer the conductor took the more fidgety she became.

"Are you going to tell me or keep me in suspense?" He chuckled. He wasn't able to fall asleep at the moment because he knew she wanted to talk.

"They are going to meet us at the train station when we arrive." She paused, waiting to see what his reaction was going to be. She hadn't told him that they were coming for a visit. She hadn't told him that in less than 90 minutes he was going to be meeting them. Maggie had thought he would change his mind about the trip if she had. Christian had given her no reason to think that, it was just her own doubts and insecurities feeding that thought.

"Wow, Maggie. That's a big surprise."

"Are you mad?"

"Why would I be mad?" He smiled. He couldn't understand where a question like that would come from. He knew she hadn't seen her parents in a long time. He also knew that although she was really enjoying her time, there were days that it was obvious that she was homesick. Christian wasn't mad at all. He was happy that she would have someone close to her that she could share this part of her life with. He felt a little tug at his heart thinking about his own family and turned to look out as the passengers were racing by the window to get to their seats on the train. He could hear the train conductor blow a whistle announcing the train was about to depart out of the station.

"I didn't tell you they were even coming for a visit, let alone hanging out with us for a couple of days," she said, watching him as he looked out the window. A woman in a long black wool coat with a white hat was running to make sure she wasn't left behind.

"Maggie, these are your parents. From everything you have ever said about them, they seem like great people. I am very happy they will be with us, I am very happy to meet them." He was speaking from the heart, although trying to hide his own nervousness. When he left the US, he had sworn to himself that he would never let anyone get close to his heart again. Letting people in meant that he would have to face his pain and past. He wasn't sure he wanted to deal with it. Now this woman was not only in his life but in his heart and later today he would be meeting her parents.

This seemed to make her relax a great deal. They were sitting side by side as the train started to pull out of the station. Christian could hear another whistle which turned out to be the final announcement indicating their departure and warning anyone near the track ahead that they were leaving the station. Maggie was looking out at the world just beyond the glass of the window. She watched as people went about the bustle of their day seemingly oblivious to the world just outside of their own little bubble. As the city started to pass by slow then picked up speed and made its way out to the countryside and on to its destination on the eastern side of this great country.

Christian was exhausted and wanted to try to get a little sleep. He looked over at Maggie to tell her his plan and realized she was falling asleep herself. To confirm this she leaned a little in his direction and then eventually laid her head on his shoulder. He was touched at this move. He knew it was a gesture of trust on her part, trust in him to keep her safe. He put his arm around her and she burrowed deeper into his shoulder, and slowly let sleep envelope her. Maggie carried the weight of the world on her shoulders which meant she was rarely at peace. As they sat there on the speeding train, Christian realized this was the first time he had seen her sleeping. After about 15 minutes of watching her sleep, fighting off his own exhaustion he noticed a peace that had settled over her that he had never witnessed with her before. It was a peace that softened her face and made her already tender features even softer. Christian said a quiet prayer to Jesus asking that He always watch over Maggie and protect her from the pain of this world and the pain from her own past that she just didn't seem to be able to let go of. As he finished his prayer, Christian felt some part of the hardness in his own heart start to melt. He realized sitting there, watching her sleep that he would do anything for her. He would do anything in his power to keep her safe. He would do whatever he could so she knew that he cared for her, that he loved her.

It was evident by his prayers that he did love her. The thought was more of a comfort to Christian than even he thought it would be. The pain that haunted him from his past kept his heart closed off for so long that he never believed it would ever open up. This woman, that was lying against his shoulder had done something to him that made all that pain seem a little less and his heart feel like he really could love again. That was the last thought he had as the train was going past the coast of Firth of Forth and Christian fell asleep himself.

CHAPTER FOURTEEN

By the time they made it to their destination, it was early afternoon. While on the train ride from Loch Grádh, Maggie had taken a short nap. When she awoke 30 minutes later, she seemed very refreshed and Christian could see excitement starting to build in her as sleep was leaving and she remembered where they were. They discussed that the first thing they would do when the train stopped was contact her parents to see where they wanted to meet up. Since what he had planned to surprise her was now out the window, he told Maggie that he was up for whatever she wanted to do. The one thing they did agree on was that after meeting up with her parents, they would make their way to a local restaurant to get some food. They were both famished from only eating a light breakfast of fruit and a piece of toast. The coffee they had both brought with them did very little to sustain them.

As they exited the train and stepped onto the platform, Maggie's eyes brightened as she looked toward the door of the station. Just below the sign indicating that they had indeed arrived in Aberdeen was a couple in their late 50's. They looked up at the sound of Maggie saying their names. They had a look of pure enjoyment themselves as they saw their daughter, whom that hadn't seen in over four months.

"Hi mom, hi dad!!" she couldn't contain her excitement any longer. She gave them both a big hug as they reached each other. They stood like that for what seemed like a lifetime before they separated and then they all dried their eyes. Christian had begun to shed a tear also. He had never known the love of a family like what he had witnessed here. He hadn't spoken to his own father in over seven years. Before that, he never had the type of relationship with him where they would never give each other a hug, let alone even act or say that he missed him. However, there, standing in Aberdeen, Scotland watching Maggie and her parents celebrate that there was no longer any distance between them was tugging at his heart even more. He was genuinely happy for her.

"Christian..." she paused, taking a moment to dry her eyes again. Her mother was taking a second handkerchief out of her purse to hand to Mr. Greene so he could dry his own eyes. "Christian, I would like to introduce my parents, Nelson and Connie Greene."

Christian reached his hand out to shake her father's hand. "It is a pleasure to meet you, sir. Maggie has said many great things about you." He said this looking at both of them.

He was very nervous but was hoping it didn't show.

"It is our pleasure to meet you as well." Mr. Greene replied.

"Maggie has said a lot good things about you." Mrs. Greene added. "Thank you for the help you have given her with her research."

Christian didn't know Mrs. Greene but the look on her face indicated that the thank you was for more than just the help on the research. Mrs. Greene was saying thank you for watching over her daughter while she was getting used to being in Scotland.

Mr. and Mrs. Greene had arrived in Aberdeen the day before Maggie and Christian. They already had their hotel room arranged at a hotel not far from the train station. They had rented a car that was parked at the end of the platform that they were all standing on. After all the departing passengers were on the train, it left the station and continued on to its next destination further north into Scotland. The day before Maggie had made arrangements at the same hotel as her parents, making the assumption that Christian would be okay with it. Up to the point that they all were getting into the rental car heading to the hotel, Christian had no clue that Maggie had made the arrangements. It wasn't evident until Mr. Greene had said that he had checked them into their rooms earlier that morning, so that they could guarantee that their rooms would be close. Christian then mentioned that he had to call the hotel where he had made a reservation and let them know he had to cancel.

Christian was sitting in the back seat with Maggie and he glanced over at her unsure of what was happening. He could only smile back at her as she sat beaming knowing that he had no clue what was going on, but happy that he kept quiet for the time being. Christian did have to laugh to himself that in all the planning he thought he had done to make this a special day for her, nothing compared to what, he was beginning to realize, she had planned for them for the next few days.

It was just about noon and they were all starting to get hungry. They drove the few blocks to the hotel. It was located in the middle of a city block that was surrounded by buildings that were over a hundred years old. Christian was trying to imagine what it would have been like a few hundred years ago, walking through these streets. Once inside, he was equally impressed as soon as they all stepped into the lobby of Stucchi's Hotel in Aberdeen. The oldness on the outside was contrasted by the modern updates to the inside looked.

Maggie and Christian were settling themselves into the hotel room talking about how they were enjoying their trip so far. Maggie had booked the room as a surprise to say thank you to Christian for all the help that he had given her on her paper. If it wasn't for him taking the time to give her the tours around Stewart Castle, she would still be at the beginning of her thesis. Now she had completed it and was working on her fact checking and rewrites.

"Are you happy with the room?" Maggie was a little concerned that Christian was upset that his plans were a bit shaken up.

"Maggie, I couldn't be happier. I am not used to someone surprising me like this but I am really enjoying myself." Christian replied as he was digging through his bag to get his personal belongings to take them to the bathroom. "Wait, are you really done with your paper?"

"The research, yes, well for the most part." Maggie smiled and then beaming at his compliment, changed the subject, "Thank you. Oh, and by the way, we have a lot of fun things planned."

Christian went to the bathroom to splash some water on his face. Maggie was sitting on the bed touching up her makeup and fixing her hair. Christian stood near the bathroom door using a towel to dry his face and hands. He watched as she ran a brush through her long blond hair. As she stood to lie her brush down on the dresser, she noticed Christian standing on the other side of the room looking at her. She blushed then turned and picked up her leather jacket off the bed. He walked over to her and helped drape the jacket over her shoulders.

"I am looking forward to whatever you have in mind to do."

"I do have one request if I may."

"Sure, if it is something I can do, I would be happy to."

"My dad is normally very quiet. If you wouldn't mind, would you talk to him and get him to open a little bit?"

It was an unusual request but Christian could already tell that her dad was a man of few words. "I will definitely do what I can to help get him to talk."

This made Maggie so happy she reached over and gave him a hug. Her jacket slid to the floor. After the hug, Christian leaned over to pick up her coat as they were finished getting ready to leave. She tied the belt of the jacket around her waist and pulled her hair out to let it cascade down her back. Christian picked up the room keys that were given to her by her dad when they first arrived. He placed one in his pocket and handed the other to Maggie as they headed out the door. They met her parents in the hallway as they were exiting their room and then the four headed out to do some exploring around Aberdeen.

They made it to the lobby of the hotel and decided to have a light, quick lunch before they headed off to see the sights. While they were eating, Mr. Greene turned to his daughter and asked what sights in the town that they wanted to see first. The small group was about halfway through their meal when Maggie offered the suggestion that they visit King's College.

This whole day, so far, had been a treat for Christian. He was seeing a side of Maggie that he hadn't witnessed prior to that day. He had seen her happy, like when she first heard the story of Loch Grádh, when she was finally able to understand Angus at The Pipers, and other times as well. He hadn't, however seen her as happy this. It made his heart lighter to see the smile she had had on her face since they left the station near his home earlier that day. Even when she was taking a nap on the train ride to Aberdeen, she slept with a smile on her face. In his heart, the feelings he had for her were growing to something much more than he ever thought he would feel again. He recognized it and did his best to control them. What future could the two of them have? He would never ask her to stay in Scotland that far away from her family and he had no desire to move back to the United States. So he kept his feelings to himself, thinking that was best for her. After they finished their lunch, Christian said a quiet prayer of thanksgiving to Jesus as they drove to the university.

~~~~~~~~~~

They drove the short distance from their hotel on Crown Street to the King's College, also known as the University of Aberdeen. Maggie had done her research and knew exactly where she wanted to start. Mr. and Mrs. Greene had no agenda and were willing to go wherever she wanted to go. Christian was used to being the one making plans, but today he was very happy to have no control and just followed the rest of the group on the way to the college. Maggie shared with them a little of the history she had found online as they were arriving to the campus. The university was established in 1495 and it was one of the top five oldest universities in all of Great Britain. It was formerly called King's College named after King James IV of Scotland and most of the locals still referred to it as such.

When they arrived they parked the car and headed toward campus. They walked through an arched pathway with a coat of arms sculpted above the arch, with the dates 1495 and 1912. The four of them stood just inside the arches gate taking in the sights.

"So where would you like to start?" Christian asked Maggie. Since it was her suggestion that they start their afternoon at the university, they all left it up to her to guide them where she wanted to go.

"Well we can walk the grounds and since I know how much you like churches, how about we start with the chapel. Then we can go to the library. How does that sound to everyone?"

Mr. and Mrs. Greene looked at each other, than at Christian. They all nodded in agreement with Maggie's suggestion. Christian was still impressed with how Maggie had been all day. Since the day they met, she had been quiet and usually willing to go with whatever the day brought. This was the first time that he had seen her this strong, this confident in her actions. He was very impressed. It occurred to him that she had to be that strong in order for her to travel to Scotland on her own to study and write her thesis.

From what she learned while doing her research, Maggie found that the oldest building on campus was the King's College Chapel. She knew that Christian's faith was the most important thing in his life and that he would want to see this building. The Chapel, like most of the old buildings on campus, was almost entirely stone. It is one of the buildings that made up the quad, which was a well manicure lawn that was used by the students on nice days to study and just gather throughout their busy days of classes.

The sky was full of clouds and threatened rain but for the time being the moisture held off. Christian was undeterred by the weather though as the pictures that he was taking were amazing. The grey skies added to the majesty of the campus and Christian was able to capture that in his photos.

Maggie was still talking about the Chapel as they walked through the main door. However, once they were inside, she didn't say much of anything. What little she did say was nothing above a whisper as she stood in awe of the grandeur of the Chapel. The woodwork that made up a good portion of the interior was said to have dated back to the medieval times and believed to be the oldest of any church in Scotland. Thinking about everything that this country had been through in its long history, it was amazing that it had lasted that long.

They spent a little over an hour in the Chapel walking around, marveling at the history they were taking in. As Americans, they weren't used to seeing something that old, that was still in use. Most old buildings in America were newer than the ones they were now looking at and had been looking at the entire time they were in Scotland. The country they now stood in held a majesty that one either understood or disregarded. Christian hadn't met too many people that were 'middle of the road' about Scotland.

They toured the grounds and a few of the buildings that Maggie had wanted to see for another two and half hours before they decided to call it a day. Everyone was exhausted and as they were headed back to the hotel, Maggie asked if there was time before they left for Loch Grádh, if they could do another quick walk around campus.

Christian could guess that it was because she wanted to compare this one to the one that she was attending back in Ann Arbor, Michigan. In reality, there was no comparison. They each had their heritage and history but they were hundreds of years apart from each other with King's College being established almost 400 years prior to the one Maggie attended. They made the short trip back to their hotel in less than fifteen minutes as Maggie and her parents discussed the progress she was making on her thesis paper. Christian was quiet as he was thinking of the Chapel and what worshipping Jesus in that building would have been like the building was first built.

~~~~~~~~~~

When they returned from their day's excursion, Christian stopped to admire the building again. The outside of the hotel looked like it was built well over 100 years ago. As interesting as the architecture of the building was though, the whole thing was lost on the beautiful purples and pinks of the picturesque setting sun. All of them stood on the walk just outside the hotel taking in the beauty of the sunset. Life in the United States was too busy to enjoy such a moment but Christian had learned to change from that way of thinking. He learned the importance of enjoying the moment, carpe diem was how he tried to live his life, and give thanks to God for all the little things He gave him. His life was much more relaxed than it ever had been back home. Christian did his best to show Maggie how to be like that was well. He had hoped that this would help her through her struggles. At first it was difficult for her because she felt like she was accomplishing more when she kept herself busy. As they stood there for a few minutes enjoying the view, Maggie took a deep breath of relaxation. Christian heard it but didn't acknowledge it because he didn't want to make her uncomfortable. Her parents heard it as well and exchanged a happy look between the two of them. It did make his heart glad to see the peace about her. She was in her early thirties and she didn't need to be carrying the weight of the world like she did.

After the sun had found its home beyond the horizon, they all walked into the lobby and agreed to go to their rooms and freshen up. They were to meet back in the lobby in about twenty minutes and have dinner in the hotel restaurant. After a quick elevator ride to their rooms, Christian and Maggie began chatting about their day.

"I think I figured out why your dad doesn't talk much."

"Really, what did you come up with?" Maggie asked, wondering how he figured it out in one day.

"I say this with no ill will, but you and your mom never give him the chance to talk."

Maggie just looked at him.

Christian was worried that he may have offended her, until she burst out laughing. He wasn't sure how to take that reaction. He was at least happy that she didn't appear to be mad.

"You are right. My mom and I can get carried away and

we never realize that we don't let him talk."

"Well at dinner I will try to get him to talk and we will see what he does."

Maggie agreed with the plan and stated that she would do her best not to answer any of Christian's questions so that her dad would be able to speak up.

The two younger Americans made it to the lobby before Mr. and Mrs. Greene did. Maggie went to the restaurant and put their name in for a table while Christian waited in the lobby for her parents. He was amazed at the transformation from the older look of the outside of the building and the rest of the block, compared to the newly remodeled inside lobby of the hotel. While he was waiting, the staff at the front desk was very friendly and helpful, giving him a little background on when the remodel had taken place. By the time Maggie had made her way back to the lobby to find Christian standing at the front desk, her parents were just stepping off the elevator.

They made their way over to the restaurant and enjoyed a good dinner with even better conversation. Christian asked Nelson a couple of questions and that sparked a good back and forth talk and Maggie and Connie just watched and enjoyed listening to him chatting. They enjoyed their dinner and a light dessert before heading back up to their respective rooms, agreeing that they would meet in the morning for the next day's excursion to a local castle.

~~~~~~~~~~

Maggie really enjoyed the castles that she had already spent time at, in Loch Grádh and in some of the outlying areas. Once they were in the Aberdeen area, she wanted to tour as many as she could, like she had been doing with Christian. The old structures held a place of awe with Maggie. Christian started to explain a few things about them but Maggie quickly stepped in and began to show to her parents all that she had learned in her short time there. Maggie's mom was very fascinated with the area and even more impressed with her daughter's knowledge of the places they visited. Mrs. Greene tried once to add a little of what she had read prior to their trip here, but Maggie, beaming, finished her mother's thought. To most, the constant interruptions by Maggie would have seemed rude but to her family, it was just how conversations went. The two did it to each other so often it had made it to the point that, at times, it was just one steady flow. It was actually quite impressive. No one was offended it was just how the two of them got along.

Christian had to laugh though. He thought of the conversation he had had with Maggie just prior to leaving the hotel room that first day they were in Aberdeen. It was obvious that her dad did have a lot to say, he just never had the chance to say it. Usually it was because he was listening to the two ladies. Christian found it endearing in a family sort of way. At first Christian thought they were acting like that to make a good impression on him, but the more he was around them the more he realized that this is how good families really are to each other. What he was used to wasn't normal. It made him happy to see that families really do get along in a loving way.

Maggie's dad was very stoic but Christian, reading Mr. Greene's body language, could tell that he was impressed and very proud of his daughter. Watching the way her parents acted around her, Christian could tell why Maggie spoke so highly of them. They were rare, in his experience of how parents treated their children. His own father couldn't care less if Christian was alive or dead. Maggie's parents were figuratively sitting on the edge of their seats listening to their wonderful daughter speak about things like what kind of stone was used for the castles, why the windows were shaped the way they were and more. These things may have seemed insignificant but to Maggie and her family, in that moment, it was important. In that moment, there was more love in that small family than Christian had experienced in his entire life with his own family.

Maggie had a way of telling a story that would draw the listener in. As she recited basic details of castle living, she gave the same information that Christian had given many times. Maggie however added emotion to the story that most people forget to add. The emotion of what she was feeling at the time, flowed from her as she told all about what it was like to live in Scotland nearly 700 years ago. She made it feel like the listener was standing right there in the castle courtyard, listening to the sounds of the marketplace as traders flowed in and out pushing their wares. The way she described the scenes, as she walked from one area of the castle grounds to another, one could almost smell the peat fires as they burned trying to dry out the dampness in the air.

Because of all the sites that Maggie and her parents wanted to see, their two and a half day trip to the east side of Scotland was stretched out to five. The only reason it wasn't more was because Christian couldn't take any more time off from work. The family had repeatedly said that they could add two more weeks to the trip and that wouldn't have been enough to see everything that they were interested in seeing in Aberdeen alone. So as they were boarding the train to head back to Loch Grádh, they vowed they would make another trip over there to see more.

CHAPTER FIFTEEN

They were all having a great time as their week progressed. They had been through a lot in the four days they had been there so far. Christian was amazed at the history of the town and of the college they had been to on day one. He was also enjoying being on the other side of the coin to where Maggie was teaching him all about the area. For never having been there, she was well informed. He wasn't sure when she had found the time to do any sort of research but he was impressed, none the less, with her vast knowledge of the area. It was even more impressive that until a week ago, she didn't even know that they were going to be visiting the seaside city in eastern Scotland.

It also fascinated Christian to see Maggie and her

parents together. He had been around her when she was talking to others, usually at The Pipers or at the castle. She would talk to those people in the casual way she did. This however was something he had never seen. With her mom, she would talk as if they were best friends. By the end of the first night, he was able to see why. They could talk about anything. If they disagreed, they would go back and forth for a few minutes then continue on with the conversation as though it had never happened. Christian was impressed with watching them talk. He had no experience with a family that could disagree and still get along, even in the same conversation. It was refreshing to see that. His own family was quite a bit different than that. This, however, was not the time to be dwelling on his family issue. In reality, that subject was no longer an issue in his life. He walked away from that the moment he walked onto the plane that flew him to the UK.

He went back to listening to Maggie and her mom. They were now discussing where they wanted to visit after they were done eating lunch. Christian and Mr. Greene looked at each other and smiled as the two of them finally narrowed down where they were going to go. They asked the two men sitting with them what their thoughts were.

"It doesn't matter to either of us," Mr. Greene answered for both of them to the delight of the women. Both men knew that the women already had in mind what they wanted to do, so they just decided to let them plan the day.

"Great," Maggie replied with overjoyed enthusiasm.

The night before, Christian took some time to rest in the hotel while Maggie spent some time alone with her parents. Christian didn't ask what they did but he could tell that they really enjoyed their evening. Maggie was talking about the conversations they had. Christian was continually amazed at how much and how easily they seemed to talk to each other. This was such a shock to him because of the experiences he had had with his own family. Maggie also mentioned earlier in their meal that she had spoken with her advisor but said that she would explain it later. For the time being, she was more focused on the plans for their last day in this beautiful part of Scotland. The place she wanted to go was somewhere that she knew her mom would thoroughly enjoy.

~~~~~~~~~~

On their last full day in Aberdeen, they decided to take the rental car and take a leisurely drive just over an hour west to Balmoral Castle. The area was the rumored spot where the Royals would spend some quiet time away from the hustle and bustle of London during the late summer and early fall time of the year. Maggie's mom was a big fan of all things British and many times had seen the travel programs that featured this magnificent area of this beautiful country. She had also mentioned to the group earlier in the week that she had read a wonderful article on how grand and open the area was. It was during their lunch conversation the day before that Christian could truly understand where Maggie had gained her fascination and love of history.

It had been agreed upon that Mrs. Greene would drive the rental car through the countryside on the way to the castle. Mr. Greene had found a comfortable spot in the back seat and had fallen asleep. Maggie navigated from the passenger seat while Christian sat behind her watching the scenery pass by. Looking at this part of the world brought a recurring memory from just before he left his job at the hospital in Toledo. One of his coworkers, trying one last time to get him to change his mind, asked him what was so nice about where he was going. The only response that came to mind was, it still looks like land held in the palm of God's hand. That statement, said with such confidence from a person who had only seen this country from photos on the internet and books, left his coworker wondering what that place must have been like to have that kind of hold on someone.

As Christian traveled through Scotland, he realized that he had been mistaken with his opinion from the pictures. Those pictures didn't do justice to the country that he was now looking at out the window of the rental, as it headed west from Aberdeen to Balmoral Castle.

When they arrived, Christian was in awe of the area. He was glad they had chosen to visit this remote area on their last full day in the northeastern part of Scotland. There were over fifty thousand acres on the estate that was once owned by Queen Victoria and Prince Albert. The interesting fact about this picturesque portion of Scotland is that Balmoral Castle is actually owned by the Royals and not the Crown, which means that no public taxes go to pay for the employees and up keep of the property.

While the group was walking around taking in the sights, each picking out the things that drew their attention, a small group of red deer ran past them less than 20 yards away. There were two does and 3 fawns that were walking to find bits of food that they could eat before running off into the woods.

Maggie removed her cell phone from her purse and did a search about the history of this estate from a site called 'wiki' something or other. She found a quote that is rumored to have come from the diary of Queen Victoria that read 'All seemed to breathe freedom and peace and to make one forget the world and its sad turmoil." It was an interesting statement by the Queen and one that Maggie was able to relate to every since she walked off the plane. The Queen was referring to Balmoral, but Maggie could attribute that to all of Scotland.

They were glad they had made it to the estate in mid June because they were still in time to walk the grounds before it was closed for the Royals to visit for their summer vacation. The foursome didn't do much talking as they walked, taking in the sites. It seemed that there were unspoken understandings that it was better to let the beauty of the area speak for itself instead of them trying to force what may have seemed like useless dialogue.

The drive back was interesting as Maggie and her mom were talking about the day and everything they enjoyed about their visit. As on the trip to the castle earlier that morning, they occupied the same seats on the return trip to Aberdeen. Mr. Greene tried to stay awake, but the car ride lulled him to sleep quicker that anyone in the vehicle could believe. Maggie had told Christian how hard her dad worked to provide for his family. The young man could understand her dad was always tired. Christian hoped that when he had a family of his own, he could be half the man Mr. Greene was for his family.

Christian, exhausted himself, watched the trees passing by and then laid his head back against the headrest and closed his eyes. At first they would ask the two men sitting in the back what they liked about the day but both of them, they noticed, had fallen asleep. The two women in the front seat couldn't contain their excitement thinking they had just spent the day at a place the Royals enjoyed as well.

As they approached the outskirts of Aberdeen, Maggie had awakened both of the men in the back and asked what they had planned for dinner. Mrs. Greene didn't even wait for either of them to answer.

"How about you two kids go and do something and Mr. Greene and I will go off and enjoy our evening."

Maggie didn't give either passenger in the back a chance to answer before she agreed with her mom. "That sounds great. There is a steakhouse that I thought Christian might enjoy, so last night I made reservations for us to eat there tonight."

"Then it is settled." Mrs. Greene said with a surety that made the two men look at each other and shrug.

"I guess we will just go along with what they have in mind." Mr. Greene smiled.

Christian just shrugged and smiled as well just as they were pulling up to the parking garage attached to the hotel.

Once having made their way into the lobby of the hotel and all having agreed upon that each pair was going to do their own thing for dinner, Maggie and Christian went to their room to freshen up as did Mr. and Mrs. Greene. When the younger couple was ready, they headed down stairs out on to the street and walked the block and a half to the restaurant that Maggie had heard about. The steakhouse had a unique name, Ye Old Cow. It made both of the young Americans laugh a little but the reviews were great. They both found out for themselves just how true they were when Christian took the first few bites of his steak and Maggie did enjoy the salmon she had ordered. Maggie did enjoy a bite of the steak he offered. Then, after eating about half of her fish platter she excused herself to the bathroom.

To his recollection, that was the first time during the

entire trip that she had done this. Christian knew that the eating disorder had its claws into her more than he knew. He understood that it was something that she would probably struggle with all her life. And there, in the steakhouse in Aberdeen, it did rear its ugly head. Maggie was in the restroom vomiting her dinner, what little she ate of it. What he didn't understand was what triggered this to happen in the last hour and a half since they had arrived back in Aberdeen. He was confused because this seemed to happen more often when she was feeling low and depressed. Over the last week, she had been the happiest he had ever seen her. Christian wanted to ask this dear woman but he wasn't sure how to bring the subject up. He knew if he pushed or put his 'clinical hat' on, she would retract into herself. If he was too casual about the way he asked, she would shrug him off.

Christian did know it was an addiction and at times addictions have no rhyme or reason for how and why they attach themselves to a certain person. He knew that everyone is addicted to something. No one was exempt from it. His whole family had struggled with an alcohol addiction at some point in their lives. Christian wasn't affected by that but he struggled with his own issue just the same. He had prayed to the Lord many times for His strength to help himself and all those he knew.

Maggie struggled with both the eating disorder and with alcohol addiction and both of them were tearing through her. The last couple of days had been a good rest for her because it didn't seem like she was struggling as bad as it normally seemed she did. Maggie hadn't carried her usually diet coke bottle with the alcohol mix since they had arrived on their little vacation. Also, as far as he could tell, she had done well with the eating disorder, until the dinner they were in the middle of there on the last night of their little vacation. He thought that maybe it had to do with Maggie seeing her parents and her not wanting them to know that she was still struggling. She was a brave woman. She did her best to face whatever demons she was facing even when they caused her to think that she wasn't worthy of being healthy.

Christian said another prayer to God that He would watch over Maggie and help her overcome this issue. He also asked His Lord to give him the knowledge and strength to help her in any way that he could. She was walking back to the table by the time he was finished praying. He was looking down at the table and hadn't noticed that she was back until she pulled her chair out and sat back down.

Christian was caught a little off guard. "I'm sorry, I didn't hear you walk up."

Maggie smiled. "Am I boring you?" She was joking with him because he was looking a little down and she wasn't sure why. He seemed like he was in a good mood prior to her bathroom trip but now it seemed that he was occupied with something in his hands.

"Not at all. Just thinking about the great time we have had this week." He knew that wasn't the complete truth but she was smiling and he didn't want to do anything to change that.

"It really has been a nice week and I am glad that we were able to do this." Maggie was gathering her coat and purse hinting that she was ready to go.

Christian paid the bill and they headed out the door and out onto the street. Once out there they decided to go for a slow walk back to the hotel. They had pleasant conversation about the fun things that they had done and the places they had visited in Aberdeen. Most of what they talked about was just small talk. That didn't matter to either of them because they were just enjoying each other's company and the quiet city streets of late evening in this eastern town of Scotland. As they walked there was nothing in the world that matter other than the two of them enjoying the moment. There were issues in both of their lives that they each struggled with but in that moment, those issues were insignificant. So Maggie and Christian just walked, enjoying each other's company. As they were talking she reached over and locked her arm in his. Christian didn't jump. He didn't flinch. All he did was pull his arm tighter against his side locking his arm a little more snug against hers.

CHAPTER SIXTEEN

As they traveled back to the south of Scotland, Maggie stayed awake and spent some quality time with her parents. Although all four of them sat near each other, Christian closed his eyes. He was exhausted and wanted to try to get some sleep. When Maggie touched his leg to see if he was awake, he didn't stir. He wanted to sleep but he also wanted her to enjoy the time with her parents. So what started out as pretending to fall asleep, turned into him actually escaping into a deep relaxing sleep, the first he had in a long time. They all had spent the last five days together and he was sure her parents would like time with just Maggie. Her parents were very kind people and Christian had an immediate connection to them. Even though they never made him feel unwelcomed, he wanted to be respectful and give them the train ride to share with just each other.

The train rambled its way back to the little town north of Edinburgh and Christian, with his eyes closed, listened as Maggie and her parents chatted about their visit up to that point. They wanted to know how she was doing, how her paper was coming along, about the cats she left back in Toledo and many other topics. At some point along the trip, he must have really fallen asleep. He jolted awake as the train pulled into the station, marking the end of their trip. He had left his car at the station at the beginning of the trip. Christian directed Mr. and Mrs. Greene in that direction as he collected their baggage and followed them over to the car park.

"Is anyone hungry?" Mrs. Greene asked after they were settled in the car and were pulling out on the main road.

"I'm famished." Maggie said. As petite as she was, she really liked to eat. Christian believed it was more because of the fellowship that came with the meals they shared than it was the actual process of eating food. She did enjoy her food though. "How about we go to The Pipers and I can introduce you to Angus." Maggie smiled at the thought. She had told her mom about the pub owner and she couldn't wait to see her mom's reaction to this genuine Scotsman.

They all agreed that an early dinner would really hit the spot. Christian turned the corner and headed towards the restaurant where Christian and Maggie had first met. Mr. Greene was sitting next to him in the front seat and Maggie and her mom were sitting in the back. Maggie was describing to her parents the day she and Christian had met. It was a short drive but her dad, tired from the trip fell asleep on the drive. Mrs. Greene enjoyed hearing the story and mentioned that she couldn't wait to meet Angus. Maggie had told her the story a few times about how the old Scotsman had given her her first taste of Scottish culture and food.

They walked into the old pub and Maggie instinctively headed in the direction of the table she and Christian normally shared. The dinner crowd was just starting to pickup but they were still able to get their seat to enjoy a nice dinner.

"Angus, these are my parents, Nelson and Connie Greene." Maggie introduced them as they made their way across the old wooden floor. Christian went ahead to the table. The fireplace was alive with a crackling fire, adding to the warmth of the temperature and the ambience of the old pub.

"Good to meet you folks." The pub owner said in his thick Scottish accent. "Good to be having you here at my establishment."

"Thank you, it is very nice to meet you." Mrs. Greene replied. The three met up with Christian as Angus took their order and went into the kitchen to get their meals started.

"Is he the only one that works here?" Mr. Greene asked. "He seems to know you guys very well."

"There is a cook that works in back and at times his wife helps wait tables but to be honest, they are rarely here." Christian paused as the thought seemed to just hit him. "As a matter of fact, I have only seen them a handful of times."

"Well he seems like a very nice person," Mr. Greene stated.

Angus brought out their food without saying a word. Maggie reminded her parents that the Scottish people are very friendly and welcoming but some, like Angus will say very little. She told her parents that they never had a lengthy conversation and that led to the mystery and intrigue of the quiet Scotsman.

As they enjoyed their meal, they decided that they were going to take the rest of the afternoon to sit and relax. Maggie's parents were going to be staying at her cottage and Christian was going to head home so they could all get some rest. Maggie knew her parents were tired from their trip, because they had been going almost since they arrived in Scotland. The rest of that day and the next day were going to be spent just enjoying the local area of Loch Grádh. Christian was going to be going into work the next day so he agreed the plan was a good one. He also knew that Maggie needed time with her parents. She had been a little sad the last day they were in Aberdeen and by the time they made it back to their hotel that last night, he realized it was because it was nearing the end of that trip and she had to get back to her normal life.

After they had finished their meal, they parted ways and agreed that they would see each other within the next couple of days. As they headed out to his car, Maggie turned to Christian and asked if he would be able to give her parents a private tour of the castle in the next few days. Mrs. Greene overheard her daughter's request and turned to see what his response was going to be.

"Of course, Maggie, you said this was your family so it would be my honor to show them around." Christian hadn't noticed that Mrs. Greene had turned but when he heard her say thank you, he turned in her direction.

"Thank you for all you have done." Mrs. Greene was beaming and in that look he could see that this was going to be the thrill of her entire trip. In reality it was Christian who was grateful to Mr. and Mrs. Greene.

Mr. Greene had stopped just short of the car and

expressed his gratitude as well. With all plans set, they climbed into his car and he drove them over to Maggie's cottage.

~~~~~~~~~~

It was a few days before Christian was able to meet up with Maggie and her parents. Since he had taken a few extra days off the previous week, he agreed to work the weekend shifts at the infirmary. They agreed that he would pick them up on Monday morning. He would take them over to Stewart Castle, where Maggie had spent the last five months working on her thesis. She was almost complete with the project and as they drove over to the castle, she asked Christian if he would mind if she led the tour with her parents. He happily agreed and when they arrived at the castle grounds, Maggie started her tour.

Christian turned back toward Maggie to see the expression on her face. She finished the tour with her parents after about an hour. She was beaming. He had seen her happy many times since they had met that night at The Pipers. This however, was the second time in two weeks he had seen her this overjoyed. Her face glowed with a radiance that was equal to looking at the sun. She knew her mom and dad were impressed, not just because of the knowledge that she had picked up since she had arrived in Scotland a few months prior. It was because this whole area was from her heritage. Her family had had a major influence on this area and she was very proud that it was a good one. Not many people know a lot about where their family came from. Even fewer knew the true history of the ancestry.

Maggie however, learned as much as she could prior to her journey across The Pond but it was nothing compared to what she gained in information once she arrived in Scotland. Christian had had a little to do with that and she expressed her gratitude many times. Initially, for Christian, he had agreed to show her around because it was his job and it would help the castle owners. However, after spending just 30 minutes with her, he continued to share his knowledge just because he enjoyed her company and wanting to spend as much time with her as he could.

Maggie escorted her parents to the edge of the loch. Christian had removed his cell phone from his pocket to take a few pictures of the three of them standing at the water's edge. The mist hovering just over the water added to the Scottish feel for the small family. Faintly, the sound of a lone bagpiper traveled across the water. Christian was able to get a picture of Maggie and her parents, as the piper played his haunting melody.

CHAPTER SEVENTEEN

It was just over a month since her parents went back to Toledo, Ohio and Maggie was in the middle of a breakdown. At first it seemed like she was going to be okay and that she wouldn't have any issues with being homesick. However, the next couple of weeks proved to be contrary to that. No matter where she turned or what she did, everything just seemed hopeless. That particular Tuesday seemed even worse. When will this storm be over, she thought? Sometimes we are our own worst enemy. Most of the time, the one that holds a person back is themselves with the negative views that they keep and never seem to be able to let go of. This is perpetuated by all the hurt and pain that they carry from all the struggles they have gone through. The better the love and support they have from those around them, the better they heal. They also learn how to be the same positive support to others around them.

The opposite is just as true. If there is not good support then even a good person can crumble under the weight of what life can throw at them. Life isn't meant to be easy, as the Bible teaches us. The only way that anyone can make it through life is by the strength of God and through Him alone. He will put people in our life to help us get through trials but in the end, it is all Him. It isn't just receiving help but also being willing to give help to those in need. This must be done without ever expecting anything in return or boasting the help that was given. When assistance is given, there should be no expectation of a reward. That selfless attitude is how God wants us to be and only that can help us get through the fires and trials of life.

Those occasions may seem rare at first, but even someone that has good support can fall also. They have love and support but the struggles of life, the weight of pain becomes so unbearable that even love doesn't seem like it will penetrate the darkness that encompasses and then tries to destroy the heart. Maggie was struggling with this and it seemed like there was no way out. She was in the middle of another breakdown at the moment and it was adding to the weight in her heart. What she couldn't see was the love that poured out of her. She was so blinded by the pain, that all the good that was in her heart went unnoticed, not by those around her, but by herself. Sadly that didn't change her perspective though.

She was tired of being in pain.

She was tired of struggling with this addiction that she knew was killing her.

She was tired of being alone.

She wanted more normalcy in her life. She wanted to feel loved. She wanted a family. She wanted to know that, even though she couldn't see much good in herself, eventually there would be something good to hold on to. Maggie just wasn't sure how to get from where she was at to where she wanted to be.

When Maggie was younger, something horrible had happened to her. She had hinted at it when she and Christian had had coffee yesterday. Now they were sitting in her living room. He was in a chair across from where she was sitting on the sofa, where she had been editing her thesis for about thirty minutes prior before he arrived. She had stopped in the middle of it and just started crying. Christian was a kind man. It had been a long time since he had had to comfort a woman, a long time since he had let anyone into his heart that he had to comfort. Maggie however, was in his life. She had found a place in his heart. So there was nothing uncomfortable about being there for this woman who was sitting before him trying and barely succeeding to hold things together. He had prayed for her many times in the short time they had known each other. She was a blessing in his life and he had hoped he was the same to her.

He said a quiet prayer to God to watch over her and heal her heart, mind, and body. It was only a quick prayer but one straight from his heart. After he finished his prayer he walked over and sat next to her on the sofa. At first, she didn't react to him sitting there. Maggie sat like a statue not wanting to break down any further. Christian gently placed a hand on hers as it rested on her leg and that was all it took for her to drop the rest of the wall and let the tears fall. He shifted so that his back was against the back of the sofa and she laid her head against his shoulder and cried and shuddered until she felt like there was nothing left inside of her. They sat like that for almost an hour without either of them having said a word.

Whatever details surrounded that incident from her childhood, she kept it locked up tight in the deep corners of her heart. Whatever it was, it kept her walled up and unable to see the beauty inside of her, the beauty that Christian could see plain as day. It was a beauty that would shine out of her if Maggie would only let her heart heal. The weight of the wall was draining her strength and on days like today, she didn't have that strength inside to keep her going. Yet she did what she could with the help of some of her vices, not realizing that those were the things that were helping to add weight to problems she couldn't seem to deal with anymore. One of her most common vices was adding a little something extra to the bottle of diet soda she kept with her at all times.

Christian had noticed it for the first time the day he had told her about the history of the castle and the loch. She sat in the pub drinking the glass of soda that Angus had brought her with her lunch. As soon as they left though, she had taken a full bottle out of her purse and began taking stolen sips of that. Fortunately, they had been so busy making their way to and around the castle grounds, she didn't drink too much of it. So he let the subject go for the time being, always meaning to bring it up another day. He noticed the busier and more distracted she was, the less Maggie would drink from the bottle in her purse. It was as if she had forgotten all about it being there. While they were together, he did his best to keep her mind occupied on other things.

It had now been over six months since that day and Christian was just now beginning to understand what was happening. Whatever it was that had happened to Maggie was continuing to tear her apart from the inside out. The alcohol that she added to her diet soda, that she used to shield herself from anymore pain, was having the opposite effect from what she had hoped. She was sliding deeper into a hole and it seemed that she didn't have any idea on how to stop it.

So he prayed. He prayed that God would give him the knowledge and patience to help her. He prayed that Maggie would see the beauty in herself and understand that those around her truly cared for her. He prayed that God would heal this woman that had made her way deep into his heart in a very short amount of time. He also prayed that God would heal her from the vices that she held on to. In the end he prayed to his Heavenly Father that His love would always reach deep into her heart.

Frustration was growing in Christian because he didn't think he was doing enough to help Maggie. He had no clue what was causing so much pain to her but all he wanted was to see her smile, wanted her to be happy. She was a sweet woman that would do anything for anyone. What was he supposed to do? With all his wishing and trying to get her to open up, he knew that he couldn't force Maggie to explain it. Nor could he make her accept his willingness to help.

~~~~~~~~~~~

She had been having a bad few weeks and as a result she didn't make much of an effort to see him. She was there on his insistence because of her struggle since her parents left. Christian had called every day since his last visit with her two weeks prior, asking if they could see each other. It was rare that they didn't spend at least some part of each day together. Against her better judgment, she graciously declined. When she was feeling the weight of the world on her shoulders, worse than normal, she didn't want to be around anyone. She believed that no one would accept her if they thought she was weak, which is how she looked at herself when she was going through her breakdown. Maggie would then use her diet cola/vodka mix to help get her through the day. She used it as a crutch without realizing it was really more of an anchor.

Earlier in the day Maggie had spoken with her mom and she was starting to feel a little better. After the phone call, she called Christian and asked if they were able to have lunch together later that day. She had felt bad declining to see him so much recently. She had gone out earlier that morning for a few groceries and now, feeling a little better, she wanted to make it up to him.

"I'm working today but if you come up to the hospital about noon, I should be able to break away for lunch. You do remember though that if things are a bit busy, I may be delayed. I will get there as soon as I can." He was acting cold and distant because she had been pushing him away over the last few weeks and now was acting like everything was okay. Deep down he was happy to be able to see her but wasn't sure why she had been so shut off recently. It really bothered him to see this woman that meant so much to him hurting the way she had been.

Maggie thought he was being a little cold in his response and almost decided to just back out of her offer to go there for a visit. She knew it was because of how she had been treating him so instead of backing out she only said, "Sounds good. I will meet you in the cafeteria. I will bring a book to keep me company until you get there."

Maybe, she thought, he really doesn't see a value in me anymore. Her heart sank at the thought. She was about to cancel her offer just as Christian answered, "See you soon." She heard the familiar beep as he disconnected the call.

Christian was genuinely happy that she was coming in for lunch. He had been concerned about her. He had tried calling her over the last few days and most of the time she didn't reply. When she did, she was vague and shut off. He was very happy to see her number show up when his phone rang a few minutes prior. She was lucky that things had been slow enough to be able to answer the call. He wasn't sure what to expect. Even though he didn't sound like it on the phone, he was pleasantly surprised when she said she wanted to meet for lunch. The rare days that he hadn't spent time with Maggie were empty. He missed her on those days more than he ever could've imagined. The thought surprised him but Christian didn't fight it. Sometimes the ache of missing someone can draw two people closer. He thought of her everyday and now he was going to see her in a few hours for lunch. Why did I act like such a jerk to her, he thought, kicking himself.

When he made it back to the nurse's station, he was informed by Phoebe, his charge nurse that his next patient was expected soon and was being flown in by helicopter. Maggie was still on his mind as he prepared the trauma room for the incoming patient. I will make it up to her when I see her at lunch. That thought made him smile as he heard the call down the hall that the helicopter had made arrived.

~~~~~~~~~~

Maggie was sitting in the cafeteria at the hospital waiting for Christian to take his lunch break. Up until a couple of weeks ago, this was becoming a regular routine for them over the last few months. She was happy to have his company and when he was at work, she missed being around him. She would never tell him because she was afraid that he wouldn't feel the same. His actions showed her that he cared for her a great deal, but she couldn't believe that it was at any serious level. Maggie knew that everyone has experienced some kind of pain and tragedy in their life that usually left them guarded. She knew Christian suffered with his own struggles but he rarely talked about it, although he was good about getting her to open up. She resisted as best as she could. Not because she was intentionally trying to push him away. She was more worried that if he knew the skeletons that she kept hidden, Christian wouldn't want anything to do with her. Maggie sat there thinking about the way things had been the last few days and it made her sad that it had taken so long for her to come out of her depression to want to leave her cottage.

This bothered her deeply because she was really beginning to fall for him and the last thing she wanted was to do anything that would push him away. Like most however, the wall that is put up to protect, was often the very thing that pushed others away. It was a sad but very real catch 22.

CHAPTER EIGHTEEN

"How are you feeling Maggie? I mean, how are you really feeling?" Christian asked after they sat back down from getting their food from the cafeteria at the hospital.

"I'm doing fine." She replied rather quickly, trying to avoid giving a real answer. Christian had learned early on that if he wanted to get an answer from Maggie about a tough subject, he couldn't ask her directly. He learned that if he didn't bring it up, she would drop her guard just a bit to open up and talk. So instead of pushing to find out how she was really doing and why she had been pushing him away the last few days, he changed the subject and started to tell her about his day.

Without revealing any specifics, he told her about one

of his patients from earlier in the morning. It was a little one that was brought in by the child's mom because the child fell while running and scraped their knee. It was deep enough that mom was having a difficult time to get it to stop bleeding. Mom was frantic as Christian had pulled the towel off the child's knee to get a good look at the injury. After doing the assessment, he placed sterile pads over the wound and went to get the doctor.

Maggie was intrigued about what he was saying and asked a few questions as Christian continued on. He told Maggie that when he walked back into the room, after the doctor had sutured the injury, to give mom the discharge instructions, he noticed that she was crying. It was obvious that she was relieved the scrape on the knee wasn't as bad as it first appeared. Neither was aware the he had entered the room, and as he was about to say something, the four year old child reached over and placed a hand on mom's shoulder to comfort her and tell her it was ok. It made mom relax and it made Christian smile. He cleared his throat to let the mother and child know he was there. He wiped a small tear as he thought of the gesture of the child trying to comfort his mother. It was amazing because the mother wanted to be the comforter to her child but ended up being the one comforted.

As Christian relayed the story, Maggie was also touched by the gesture of the child. It made her remember that no matter how much bad was in the world, there was even more love and kindness. It usually went unnoticed because they appeared in smaller actions. She was also impressed because his actions showed her just how much of a caring person he was. That was all it took and Maggie started to open up and tell him everything that was going.

"I am not sure what is happening to me" she started to say, "but the last few days, I feel completely alone."

Christian wasn't sure what she was getting at and he was hoping that it had nothing to do with him trying to include her into his life over the last few months. Then he wanted to kick himself for being selfish making it about him when she was trying to tell him what was going on. So, without saying anything, he took a drink of water and let her continue at her own pace.

"I know there are things about my past that I have never told you. Things that I feel that if I did tell you, you would run for the hills. I know that I do not want that to happen so I have kept a lot of things locked up. That in turn pushes those I care about away."

Maggie was making perfect sense and Christian was glad to hear that she was realizing what was happening. Still, he sat quietly and let her continue.

"It seems like forever," she paused not sure if she should continue or not. After a brief moment she did, "but I have been suffering with bulimia for the last 15 years." Again she paused, looking for any sign that he was going to be judgmental toward her like so many others had been throughout her life. To her surprise, he just sat there listening intently to what she was trying to say, albeit very slowly.

Christian wasn't surprised by this. From his experience as a nurse, he knew the signs of when people were trying to tell him something that was important and could help in their care. He knew to just be quiet, let them talk, and he could pick through and find the relevant information. With Maggie he had been able to read the signs of her pain almost from the beginning of the friendship. However, he knew that there had to be more to the story. Christian knew that one does not simply wake up and decide that they want to have an eating disorder. What made him a good nurse was that he believed that a good medical professional didn't just treat the symptoms. They did what they could to find the source of the problem and start to treat that. In Maggie's case, the eating disorder was only a symptom and so was the alcohol. He was waiting for her to finish what she was saying, hoping that she would reveal the source. However, she glanced at her watch and realized that Christian needed to get back to work as his lunch break was over.

Christian realized why she had stopped and was a little frustrated. She had begun to open up and then the door was slammed shut because his lunch hour was over.

Maggie looked a little relieved. Partly because she was able to open up a little and finally tell this kind man sitting next to her that she suffered with bulimia but also because she didn't have to tell him any more than that, at least for the time being. Of course that meant that she was able to feel safe a little while longer. She also knew him well enough to know that his having to go back to work was just a temporary speed bump in her story. Maggie knew she had to prepare herself to be ready to tell him the rest of the story the next time they were together. To her surprise, she wasn't as afraid of the thought as she first imagined she would be.

They got up from the table and Maggie gave him a long hug and quietly whispered "Thank you' in his ear. He smiled, didn't say a word, and went back to the ER to finish his shift, leaving Maggie feeling a lot better than she had in the last few weeks.

CHAPTER NINETEEN

When Christian first arrived in Scotland, he knew there was going to be a lot of things that were different that he would have to get used to. Most of them were things he was really looking forward to taking on. One thing that he hadn't really thought of, was how he was going to celebrate Christmas. He had committed his life to Jesus years ago. Growing up he celebrated the winter holiday like most, with shopping, gifts, etc. However he knew the best part of Christmas was the celebration of the birth of Christ. He had many friends that celebrated the season in their own way which was nothing more than a variation of what he was used to. None of that ever prepared him for the way this holiday was celebrated here, in his new home.

Snow had started to fall the previous day and still hadn't let up by the time Christian was leaving for his job at the castle. Even though winter was still a month and a half away, the falling snow indicated that it wasn't going to wait. It wasn't a heavy snowfall. It was more on the side of flurries that continued to fall. Fortunately the ground was still warm enough that most of it had melted instantly when it hit the ground. Living in the Midwest of the United States prepared Christian for cold, irrational weather. No matter how much he was used to it back there, he was not longer a fan of snow and the cold. The only time he was ok with snow was at Christmas and the season leading up to that day. On this snowy morning, there on his way to work, it was beginning to look like his second favorite holiday. There was a row of evergreen trees that lined the pathway that led up to the castle. The branches were lightly dusted with a powdery white snow. The image reminded him of Christmas as a child and the way his grandparents hung paintings of wintery scenes around their home.

It was the beginning of November. When he arrived inside Stewart Castle to start his shift as tour guide, he noticed his coworkers were gathered in the foyer. Rarely were all the tour guides there at the same time. They all worked part time and usually had staggered hours. The entryway was where his supervisor Iain McClellan had gathered Christian and his four other co-workers, Katie, Ian, Stacy, and Brenda to have a meeting to discuss how the castle would be decorated that year for the holiday season celebrating the birth of Jesus. Christian was excited to hear that because although it was his second favorite holiday, Christmas was his favorite time of year. There was a magic about it that reached into the heart of everyone and made them feel young again, if only for a short time that is.

Not all of the castle was open to visitors and Iain informed them that they were only going to decorate the common areas which consisted of most of the main floor and part of the upper floor. In those areas, the owners requested that there be a lot of candles and evergreen garland scattered throughout. The rest of the decorations for inside were up to the workers.

Outside, the main courtyard would be decorated with greenery and white lights. In some places there would be candles. The rest would be the small twinkling lights, thousands of them. The lighting would line the driveway. Christian was looking forward to how the castle would look that Christmas.

The staff was very excited and responded to Iain with many questions on who would get what room, when were they to start and what was the deadline to have everything finished. Iain, as patient as he always appeared, answered the barrage of questions to the staff's happiness. After the meeting was finished, everyone left knowing what their direction was and what areas they would be taking care of and all seemed equally excited for the assigned task. This was the highlight of the local area. They would have upwards of 500,000 visitors between the second week of November and the second day of the New Year. The owners, Cailean and Marcail Stewart were very proud of the tradition of making the castle a warm, enchanting place for people to visit during that time of year.

Christian was the last of the employees to leave the castle grounds after the meeting. He and Iain walked out to their respective vehicles together. When Iain had told them during the meeting that they would have a week to complete the decorations, Christian had a great idea enter his head. Now that they had a minute to chat alone, the American would share that thought with his boss.

"Would you mind if I brought a friend in to help me decorate my area?"

"Are you not confident of what you will be able to do?" Curious as to why his American worker would be asking such a question.

"I think I could do a satisfactory job." He replied, adjusting the ball cap on his head that he wore almost every day. The logo on his hat revealed his favorite sport and team in hockey.

"I agree. The owners noticed the help you have given around the property and they have has been impressed. I must say, I have been as well."

Christian wasn't used to hearing praise. So he politely said thanks and then continued on with his thought. "Do you remember meeting my American friend?"

"Of course, she is a descendant of the family here. Are you asking if she would be able to come here and help?" Taking an educated guess at what the young American was trying to get at.

"I know she would appreciate the offer. She has been very thankful for you letting her get some of the behind the scenes information for her paper." Initially, Christian wasn't sure that Iain would allow Maggie the access to information for her paper. His supervisor made a comment hoping that this American wasn't after sort of fame or glory from the owners. When he met the woman, Iain's fears were put aside as he was impressed with her character and her story of why she wanted to use her heritage for her thesis. He realized very quickly that she was genuine and had given her permission to anything she needed.

"I would be very happy if she helped. I believe the owners would be happy also. They have spoken of her many times and are impressed with what she was trying to accomplish with the paper she is writing. You have my permission and speaking for them, their permission as well." Christian had met the owners many times and felt like he had a good report with them.

Christian was overjoyed to hear his answer. They wished each other a good evening and got in their own car. As Iain drove out of the parking lot, Christian sat and made a quick phone call to Maggie asking her to meet him for an early dinner.

~~~~~~~~~~~

It had been a few weeks since Maggie and Christian had met for lunch at the Royal Infirmary of Loch Grádh. They had spoken just about every day since and with the exception of one day and then they were back to seeing each other almost daily. Maggie had really let Christian into her heart and realized that he would not intentionally hurt her and therefore she didn't have anything to fear. She could tell by his genuineness that he did have her best interest at heart. Even if it had only been a short time since the day they had met for lunch and she opened up about her eating disorder, she didn't feel like she had to walk alone through the darkness of her past, well part of her past anyway. There was still more she needed to tell him but didn't know when or if she could open up that much yet. There was, however a deepness about their relationship that she had never experienced before. No matter how good it felt, there was still that little whisper of her past that threatened to overtake her if she dropped her guard. It was a daily struggle that she felt one day she would eventually lose to.

When Christian called and asked her to dinner, even though she was always struggling, she held on to the happiness she felt when her phone first started to ring and she noticed it was him. She held on tight with both hands and in that moment, Maggie refused to let go. It was an easier task than she had expected because of the sound of excitement in his voice when she finally said hello into the phone.

After a few minutes of small talk, she couldn't contain her own excitement any longer, "ok, ok are you going to tell me why you are so excited?"

Without giving up any information, "Nope, I will tell you when we meet up for dinner. Are you available to meet me soon?"

"Really?" she played along, "you are going to torture me?" She was smiling knowing that she wasn't going to get anywhere but having fun as they chatted. While she waited for him to answer, she started getting ready to leave, gathering her purse and coat and stopped in the bathroom to fix her hair.

"You will find out soon enough." That was all Christian was going to tell her until they met at The Pipers. They agreed that they would see each other in less than a half an hour and disconnected the call, leaving Maggie to wonder what was going on. They both quickly finished getting ready and headed out their respective doors to head out to an early dinner.

They both arrived at the restaurant at the same time, which was ten minutes earlier than they had planned and walked through the big oak door together.

~~~~~~~~~~

As he suspected when he extended the invite to Maggie less than 30 minutes ago, The Pipers Pub wasn't very crowded when Christian and Maggie met for an early dinner. It was funny that neither of them were tea drinkers prior to their arrival in Scotland. It was something both just picked up on and now were enjoying tea and biscuits during their regular meetings. Christian was putting a little cream in his tea and Maggie placed one cube of sugar in hers. They had both tried a few different combinations before they settled on how they enjoyed it on their usual meetings.

"You will never guess what happened at the castle today." He was teasing her with the question knowing that she wouldn't be able to guess. However, his excitement could not be contained and he made no effort to try.

"I don't know. Hopefully it was something good." Maggie smiled above the tea cup that she was bringing up to her mouth. She blew across the top of the tea to cool it off a bit before she took a sip.

"We are going to be decorating the castle and the castle grounds for Christmas. They have a standard base they want us to use but the rest of it is up to those of us who work there." He paused for a moment wanting to build the suspense, then he continued, wanting to explain why he was excited about it. "I spoke with my supervisor and with the permission of the owners, they unanimously agreed."

Maggie was caught off guard with what he was implying. "Are you saying what I think you are saying?"

He knew just how excited she would be to help decorate

the castle for Christmas. "Of course I am. Are you up for it?" Christian knew that Maggie was having issues lately. She was making an effort to keep herself together. Maggie didn't have much to occupy her mind and time because her thesis was almost completed. She had a little left to edit and rewrite but the research and writing were finished. She had never did get a part time job which was initially part of her plan when she moved there. All she had in Scotland was her quiet time in her cottage, her few acquaintances she had met and all the time she spent with Christian. She had been depressed and he had been trying to find something that might lift her spirits. When his boss at the castle agreed to this, he knew that this would help.

Maggie wasn't sure what to say at first. She was her own worst critic and it was a difficult task for her to believe that anyone would care what she thought or had to offer. Whenever she was with Christian, it seemed that he was always doing things for her, to make her happy. It didn't matter what was going on, it just always felt that she was first on his mind. Just like with this new thing he presented her with, the two of them were going to be decorating a room in an authentic Scottish castle, a castle that was from her heritage, for Christmas. Maggie couldn't believe this was really happening. This realization into what he was saying sunk in and she started beaming.

Maggie was struggling in some aspects of her life but overall, she was really starting to feel at home in Scotland. Even with her research, she had adapted better than she ever would've thought she could have. Christian helped this by all he was trying to do to make her feel more comfortable. He included her in as much as he could. Maggie was thrilled at this chance and she didn't want to do anything that would cause anyone to be disappointed in her. Christian could see a dark cloud of self doubt start to form in her eyes. He didn't want her to lose the happiness that was there just a moment before.

"Iain was thrilled when I asked for permission for you to help me," he said, trying to get her to focus back on that happiness.

Maggie just looked at him for a moment, the dark cloud hovering for a brief instant longer. "Thrilled?" Maggie asked. She paused, then, her radiant smile broke through, "I can't imagine Iain ever showing that he was thrilled about anything." She started laugh   ing at the thought of the very stoic Iain showing that he was thrilled.

Christian was caught off guard. He looked at Maggie and then started to laugh as well. He had known Iain for two years and he was the most proper, never wavering man Christian had ever met. Christian was happy that Maggie was making the effort to grab onto her happiness.

When her parents would praise her for something, she believed they said it just because they were being good parents. However, when others would praise her for anything, she had a difficult time believing that it was even remotely genuine and couldn't take it to heart. Over in Scotland, she found that people were very polite and seemed very genuine. She knew that Iain and the Stewarts were taken with her and she was slowly beginning to understand that she wasn't a horrible person and maybe, just maybe the compliments were true to heart.

After she finally came to terms with the compliment, she brightened and said "I would love to." After she made it to that point, she let the compliments sink in, the ideas just started to come to her on what she thought would work best in the room they were assigned to decorate. The room that had been assigned to Christian and Maggie was the last room that the visitors would see as they ended their tour. This was considered the honored room because it was the room they would remember the most. It was the one that would keep the visitors talking and hopefully wanting to return and bring more of their family and friends with them.

When the fear of failing subsided, her strengths shined forth. When that happened, Maggie's smiled brightened and Christian could see the excitement starting to rise in her. In classic Maggie style, she turned all business and asked, "Do you know what the parameters are?" She wanted to make sure that her growing list of ideas was within the vision that the Stewart family wanted to represent their home.

"The theme is a traditional Scotland Christmas, with nothing gaudy."

"I have so many ideas that would work. When I was young, my mom taught me how to do classic decorating for Christmas. As I grew up, we would decorate every room in our house every year, with one room in particular decorated in honor of our Scottish heritage." She chuckled to herself because she never thought that all the things that she had learned growing up about Christmas would be put to good use until now.

Christian had planned to only have a quick dinner to tell her the good news. Two hours later they were still sitting at The Pipers discussing the plans for the room. It was almost another hour by the time they decided to leave as dinner rush in pub was in full swing. Christian was about to ask his friend if she was ready to go but Maggie was already getting up and gathering her things. He took that as the answer to his unspoken question. She was quiet as they made their way to the door. Maggie was so focused on her new project she barely heard Angus holler out a good evening wish to her and Christian as the two of them left the pub. The elder pub owner was not offended though because she had been quiet the whole time the two of them were sitting there. He was overjoyed that Christian had found a way to give her the chance to do this new project. Angus knew she needed this to focus on.

Maggie suggested they do everything they could to keep the entire room in a classic Scottish feel, deciding to do no decorations that they wouldn't have had one hundred years ago. It was a great idea because Christian was not a fan of the gaudy decorations that were being delivered from the Far East. Since she had the experience to do a traditional Scottish Christmas, he didn't feel the need to go over the details again of what the Stewarts wanted. What he did say to her was that the decorations should be made in Scotland or somewhere in Great Britain or they shouldn't use them.

Christian was happy with the ideas that Maggie had come up with and even more impressed that these were ideas just off the top of her head. When she drew up a rough draft of what the room could look like, she quietly waited for his opinion. "Well that should be perfect. We will get started tomorrow. Tonight we can go to the market and see what we can find. Is that ok?" This was agreed on since most of the three hours they were at The Pipers was spent on the details of that original idea.

As they were walking through the market, Christian asked her, "How is your thesis paper coming along?"

Maggie took a deep breath, showing him that that was part of the source of her issues lately. "It is almost finished," and that was all she said.

"Well that is good news," Christian paused, "isn't it?"

"It is," Maggie wasn't sure how to continue, "but the deal for me coming here was that as soon as I was finished I would have to go back home to the United States."

And there it was, Christian thought to himself. She finally told him what the current issue was. Maggie reached into her purse and pulled out her bottle of diet soda. Christian had turned away looking at something on the shelf and noticed her putting the bottle back in. Christian was disappointed but didn't want Maggie to see the look on his face, but had failed. There was disappointment on both of their faces as they stood in the market shopping for decorations for their project at the castle.

Christian took a step towards Maggie and embraced her. She was shivering as he hugged her and he knew that it was not due to the cold outside.

"Maggie, I completely understand what you are going through, well at least part of it anyway. I am here if you need me for as long as you need me."

Maggie didn't say anything but lowered her head onto his shoulder. "Want I need, what I want is to be loved."

Christian's heart broke when he heard that. He had spent all the time with her that he could. He thought that everything that he was doing was showing her respect as a person, as a woman. He did love her, and it took that moment standing in the market in Loch Grádh Scotland for him to understand that. She was someone that he had searched his entire life to fall in love with. What was going on with him that he was unable to drop his wall enough to love her and to let her know it? Why does the past do everything in its power to destroy that future for those that only want hope of something better?

"Maggie, I have done my best to be respectful of you and everything you have on your plate. There is so much going on that the last thing I wanted to do was to ever be a source of stress for you."

Maggie lifted her head and pulled away from him in order to look at him as he spoke. This made Christian feel even more awkward as it was finally his turn to really open up to this wonderful woman.

"I will be honest with you, I did all of that," he took a deep breath searching for the right words, "not out of any obligation but because from the moment you walked into the pub that evening so many months ago, I had fallen in love with you."

Maggie wasn't sure what to say but Christian did get his answer when she looked up at him, smiled deeply in her eyes and gave him a kiss standing right there in the market.

CHAPTER TWENTY

Two weeks later the decorating was finished. Not just the room that Maggie and Christian had been assigned to, but all the rooms that Iain had assigned to the entire team at Stewart Castle. All the tour guides and their helpers were assembled in the kitchen of the castle that doubled as the employee break room while they were working. Iain had assembled the team thirty minutes prior to opening for Day One of the Christmas tour. It was now the beginning of December just weeks before Christmas Day and the atmosphere around the room was teeming with holiday spirit.

The group huddled in the kitchen was excited about the opening evening of Christmas time at the castle. They were expecting a big crowd so Iain made sure they were all there to work. He was hired twenty years ago by the Stewart family and he knew what to expect when the crowds were at the door on this wonderful day. Christmas at Stewart Castle was one of the area's biggest attractions during the Christmas season in eastern Scotland. They could have upwards of a half a million people come through those big oaken doors that were the entrance to the historic building. The Christmas event at the castle would last through Christmas and up to New Years day. The party that was celebrated to bring in the New Year was the highlight of those that were lucky enough to be invited. To sing 'Auld Lang Syne" standing in the large banquet room in front of the crackling fire was sight to behold.

Maggie was nervous as she stood just behind Christian as they were in the kitchen waiting for Iain to begin the meeting. She was uncomfortable to be standing in the midst of this group that were there to acknowledge all the hard work everyone did to get that place ready. There was a lot of energy in room, to the point where there was very little talking. Sensing that Iain was about ready to talk, the butterflies in her stomach took flight and she took a step toward Christian for comfort and security. Her shoe squeaked on the tile as a hush settled on the rest of the group. Maggie searched for her comfort drink but Christian put his hand on her arm to deter her from finishing the movement as she had finally found the bottle in her purse. She gave into his urge for her to not take a drink and dropped the bottle back in. He was proud of her that she had been able to resist the temptation, even if it was just for a moment. Christian put his hand on her back as she moved closer to him waiting for Iain to start the meeting. She was standing so close, Christian could feel her nervous breath on the back of his neck.

"Thank you everyone for coming in early. I must say that all the rooms turned out to be more elegant than anyone could have guessed. Without even trying or any preplanning, everyone chose a classic Scottish feel." He paused as was his style. He knew never to use many words when a few would work better.

The group all looked at each other. This was the part of the meeting where Iain would announce who won the best decorated room. He would award the winner with a night at any restaurant they wanted either in Loch Grádh or in Edinburgh. The way the group was on their toes, waiting for the winner to be announced, one would think they were giving out a bag of gold. Yet it wasn't the prize that kept everyone in the room waiting to hear. It was the thought of knowing they helped make a Christmas event for the visitors that drove them to do a great job. This particular year was different than previous years. Iain was just about to make his announcement when two members of the Stewart family walked in the door. Mr. Stewart nodded for the long time employee to continue.

"This year, everyone is a winner. Mr. and Mrs. Stewart had such a difficult time deciding who would win because they were all done so well, they determined that everyone would share the prize." The Stewarts had very kindly awarded the night out to all the employees that worked at the castle for doing such a great job. Iain handed out the gift certificate envelopes to all the staff. They were then encouraged to open them before they went out to their rooms and the visitors allowed to enter in for the tour. Inside was a gift certificate for each worker that generously covered each person and their entire family. There was also a Christmas bonus to say thanks to each of them.

~~~~~~~~~~~

The two Americans were enjoying the Christmas season more than they could ever remember having so before. They used the gift certificate to go to a restaurant in Edinburgh that Maggie had read about and thought that she would really enjoy eating at. It made Christian smile to think that this woman liked to eat as much as she did. He had said many times that he, if it wasn't for survival, would never eat. Like Maggie, he really enjoyed the fellowship of sitting and enjoying a meal with someone or many people but when it came to the eating portion of it, he only did that to survive.

The restaurant that Maggie picked out was a place that was known mostly by the locals. It wasn't one that had the draw of tourists visiting the historic city. That was one of the things that made her want to go there. She wanted to go walk around the town early in the evening and then enjoy a quiet dinner with the man she was growing even closer to. Maybe it was the time of the year, she wasn't sure, but over the last week and a half, she could tell that things were going good between them.

As they walked and looked at the city in full life with Christmas decorations and snow falling, Maggie pulled her overcoat close around her. Christian was walking beside her and had his arm around her. They walked past a gift shop that Maggie wanted to go in to look for something to send back to her parents. They walked in and the little bell above the door rang to announce their entry into the cozy shop. Maggie walked away from Christian once they were inside and had shaken off the cold. She was off to do some shopping.

Christian stayed a good distance away and watched her. She was very thoughtful as she gathered up a few things that she knew that her family would thoroughly enjoy.

They finished up at the shop and made their way to the restaurant. As they sat down Maggie was looking at the menu. "I think I may have a glass of wine," she said looking down at what she may want to eat.

"That sounds good," Christian said, but he knew that really wasn't what he wanted to say.

Maggie could tell that he was disappointed and that was the last thing she wanted on this very special night for the two of them.

"Maggie, I am not your boss. You do whatever you want. Just make sure it is not going to be something that you will regret." That was all Christian said on the subject.

"A glass of wine has never been the issue. It is usually the harder stuff that will do me in. I am not going to be drinking anything like that tonight."

Christian smiled and changed the subject. "You know, I think I am going to have a steak. What sounds good to you?"

Maggie took his lead and agreed that she wanted a steak as well.

When the waitress arrived at their table to take their order, they both ordered their steaks and side orders. Maggie was caught completely off guard when he ordered drinks for both of them. He ordered a glass of water and a glass of red wine for himself and a glass of pinot grigio for her.

Before the glass of wine arrived, she was more relaxed than she thought she would be and they sat and enjoyed the rest of their dinner. The drive home was very relaxing as well as they enjoyed pleasant conversation for part of the ride and then as she was getting a little tired, she laid her head on his shoulder and fell asleep.

CHAPTER TWENTY-ONE

Snow had been falling for the last two days. It had blanketed the field outside the cottage where Maggie was staying. In a strange and happy bit of irony, the cold of the air, the snow on the ground warmed her heart that only the love of celebrating the birth of Jesus could bring. She had really wanted to draw closer to Him but was never really sure how to accomplish that. Somehow, Christmas time made it easier. Being reminded that Jesus left His throne in heaven to bring His children closer to Himself was one of the best ways to continue developing a relationship with Him.

When Maggie first arrived in Scotland she started having her morning tea and breakfast on the porch that faced the open field to the back of the cottage. That morning it was too cold to sit out there, so Maggie sat at the table next to the window. She was watching the growing deer stroll around the field near the porch as if she was looking for her friend to share her breakfast with her. Maggie has enjoyed spending the summer with this little woodland creature that would show up almost every morning.

Maggie sat at the table after she finished eating. She started to go over her list to make sure that she had everything to make the dinner that she had planned for Christian the next day. This was going to be her first attempt at making a complete Christmas dinner for someone special. Many times Maggie had helped her mom back in Ohio, but never did the entire thing on her own.

Ever since the time they spent decorating the castle, things between Maggie and Christian had been going very well. Christian had accepted the invitation to spend his Christmas with her. She was very happy with that because he had spent the last three days in a row working at the Royal Infirmary and she knew that he needed some time to relax. In addition, she didn't want him to stay home on Christmas. She really wanted to make sure that she made him a dinner that would hopefully make him feel at home. So she sat and went over her list to make sure that everything was in order.

~~~~~~~~~~~

Maggie and Christian had spent more than ten months together. It had been some of the best memories of her life. They did a lot of things together and over the course of that time they grew closer. It wasn't the big things they did, like their trip to Aberdeen that meant the most to her. It was the quiet times they just sat and talked. Whether it was sitting at The Pipers or walking around the grounds of Stewart Castle, she enjoyed being with him. It didn't matter to her if she was talking to him about her life back in northwest

Ohio or listening to Christian about his days at the Infirmary. Maggie was even happy the times when they would sit in silence along the banks of Loch Grádh, watching the ducks splash around without a care in the world. Even though her skeletons that haunted her past did their best to destroy her, her growing faith in Jesus was stronger and she did her best to focus on that. She failed at times throughout the day and then she would end up taking a drink of her diet soda mix.

As Christmas day dawned, Maggie was busying herself around her rented cottage getting everything ready for her guest to arrive. She had invited Christian because she wanted to say thank you for all his kindness. Well the reality of it was, she had fallen for him a long time ago. Being that Christmas was her favorite holiday, she couldn't think of anyone else that she wanted to spend this day with other than Christian. Their relationship had blossomed into something more than anything she could've imagined and Maggie had hoped that Christian had felt the same. In a couple of hours, she would know for sure because she planned to open up and tell him how she felt. Maggie was nervous but she had to take the chance. Sure he had told her that he was falling in love with her but she doubted it because she still wasn't sure how to take a compliment.

For now, Maggie had to focus on preparing the Christmas dinner for the two of them to enjoy. If she distracted herself with anything else, anxiety would take hold and she would find every reason she could to cancel the dinner. Maggie already knew she would be fighting an uphill battle. She loved to eat but no matter how good the food tasted, she struggled with the eating disorder. Today was not the day that she wanted to be dealing with those issues. She wasn't going to deal with the bulimia and she wasn't going to deal with any anxiety or so she had hoped.

Today was about exactly that, hope.

Today was about a better future.

Today was about celebrating the birth of Jesus.

As she worked in the kitchen getting the dinner together, the smell of the roast turkey filled the entire cottage. It reminded her of the time when she had Christmas with her family. The twinkling lights there at the cottage were from the lit candles she had placed around the living room and dining room. She had placed a live small evergreen tree long the wall that separated the two rooms. It was decorated with more of the little white lights and a small lit star on the top. The whole cottage gave off a very warm feel that added to the wonderment of the day.

The antique clock on the wall chimed one o'clock as she removed the small turkey from the oven to baste it one more time. Christian would be there any time. Maggie had told him to be there around one thirty but he was always early, to a fault, and she knew he would be knocking at the door at any moment. She did a quick look around at all she had done to prepare the meal and the cottage. Satisfied she turned to go to the bedroom to freshen up, when she jumped at the knock on the door. He's here she thought, and I look horrible. The nervous young woman paused to look in the mirror hanging on the wall next to the cozy chair where she had spent many nights, working on her thesis, under a warm blanket with a fire crackling in the fireplace. She fussed with her hair for a moment then shrugged.

"He will like it or not, but there is nothing I can do about it now." Maggie sighed as the words barely escaped. She took a deep breath to settle her nerves. When that didn't work, she put on a nervous smile and then opened the door to greet her guest.

~~~~~~~~~~

He knew a thing or two about building walls, closing doors, burning bridges and all that went with keeping people at a distance. He had his share of hurt that caused him to not only keep those doors around him closed but he kept walls behind those closed doors just to make sure. For all the pain he had been through, all the times his heart had been broken, he was determined to keep the pieces of his heart just that, pieces. Christian knew that there was nothing in the world that would heal his heart back to whole again. It may sound illogical to some but if the pieces were never put back together, then there was no chance that it would ever break again. A broken heart can only be broken so much, right? His heart had been broken so many times that it was more comfortable to stay like that than to keep fighting an uphill battle to try to keep it whole.

Christian was running from his past. Like everyone, he had his share of pain, his share of heartache. It was too much for him to bear on most days. When the opportunity to go to Scotland fell into his lap, he grabbed it with both hands. When he thought of his past, it reminded him of his father. Everything that Christian disliked about himself reminded him of the man he grew up with. Once he was older, he did everything in his power to be as different from him as he could be. The problem with running from his past was that the past is not a location on a map. His past was in his head and in his heart. No matter how much he ran, he could never escape or hide from those. Love was the only thing that would heal him and it was a love that only Jesus could provide. Christian realized that he had to heal if he ever wanted for him and Maggie to be close. He had to face his fear. He was having dinner with her that evening and he wanted to tell her how he felt, in depth.

Christian had paced the floor for twenty minutes before he put on his brown loafers and went to the closet to find the jacket he was going to wear when he headed over to Maggie's. His small flat on the edge of town was feeling very confining at the moment. He realized it was because of how nervous he was feeling. The problem was, he didn't know why he was feeling so nervous. In both of his jobs he was used to meeting people. He was outgoing enough so that never made him feel uncomfortable. He tried to live his life in a way that would honor Jesus. So he welcomed everyone that came into his life the best he could. Maggie and Christian had spent a lot of time together. So he didn't understand why, as he was getting ready to spend the day in celebration of the birth of Jesus with Maggie, that he was feeling so nervous. He couldn't take it any longer and since he didn't have an answer, he put his coat on and headed out the door.

The day was cold but nothing he wasn't used to. Although the weather man said they should expect another couple of inches of snow later in the overnight hours, Christian decided to walk the two miles to Maggie's cottage. It had stopped snowing at the moment and the roads had already been cleared as the county officials wanted to make sure they were okay for safe passage for those that would be traveling that day.

Christian put on his headphones to listen to one of his favorite Christian bands that was loaded on the music player on his phone. The music was soothing and helped to calm him down. When he neared her place, his hunger was growing, so he knew that he was over the nervousness. However, by the time he was on her street only two houses away, he could smell the dinner she had been making earlier that day. When he knocked on the door, his stomach was growling. None of that mattered when he opened the door and noticed the beauty that was on the other side of the threshold.

At first he didn't respond when she opened the door and invited him in. His breath and voice were caught in his throat. Maggie thought there was something wrong with her hair, her outfit, her makeup, something in her teeth. They stood on either side of the door frame for what seemed like an eternity.

"Welcome, come on in and make yourself at home." Maggie repeated her invitation, thinking that maybe Christian hadn't heard her the first time.

Christian barely snapped out of his trance and "Thank you," was all he could manage to say. Even then it was more of a reaction than any actual effort. She looked even more beautiful in that moment than anyone he had ever seen before. The flickering glow from the candles behind her made her look more radiant than he could've imagined. He stood on the porch, speechless. Maggie had said something to him. Christian wasn't sure what it was but he was through the door before he even realized his feet were moving.

"Are you okay?" Maggie asked, the concern in her voice bringing him back to reality.

"I'm fine." He finally caught his breath. "I am fine. I was just in awe at just how beautiful you look today." His voice trailed off as he watched her glide across the floor and head to the kitchen. It was almost as if she floated like an angel.

Maggie was uncomfortable, at first, by his compliment. She knew him and knew that it was not an empty sentiment trying to make her feel good about herself. This impressed her and she knew it was genuinely from his heart.

"Thank you," she replied sheepishly. "I have been working in the kitchen all morning and really don't believe that, but thank you."

Things were finally starting to settle a bit and he placed his coat on the hook near the door. The aroma of the food emanating from the kitchen at the back of the cottage, reminded him of just how hungry he was. Not wanting to seem too eager to jump into eating, he stopped to look around at the decorations that Maggie had placed around to liven up the cottage for Christmas. He had only visited her in the cottage a handful of times. She had done a wonderful job bringing the spirit of the season to life around her Scottish home.

Maggie noticed Christian looking around the place. "I did this right after we finished at the castle." She smirked a little and added, "What can I say? I was in a decorating mood."

Christian returned her smile, "Well you did a great job here, just like you did at the castle." Maggie blushed and then motioned for him to have a seat in the living room. From there he would be able to watch her as finished their Christian meal. Softly, in the background, he could hear Christmas music playing. Her heart felt light and she knew it was going to be an enchanting evening. She turned to head into the kitchen to start gathering food to bring to the table for them to eat.

"Is there anything I can do to help?" Christian usually

spoke with a soft voice that usually put her at ease. Thinking he was sitting in the living room, it actually made her jump when he spoke as he was right behind her.

"Sure," she said, her heart still beating fast from being startled. "How about you remove the turkey from the oven and carve it?"

"Sounds good," he said as he grabbed a pair of oven mitts off the counter and reached to open the oven door.

CHAPTER TWENTY-TWO

"Dinner was delicious," Christian said as he leaned back in his chair and let his stomach start to digest the meal he had just spent the last 45 minutes enjoying.

Maggie was happy to see him relaxing. He was always so stoic and rigid. It was nice to see this relaxed side of him. Maggie really wanted to talk to him about how she felt but was unable to figure out a way to fit the subject into the dinner conversation. Instead both shared some of the favorite memories of Christmas from when they were younger. Christian talked about a time when his grandparents came from Tonawanda New York to his childhood home in southeast Michigan. Those visits were more of a highlight than getting presents. He shared that his grandfather would sing "Leon" instead of "Noel" to one of his favorite Christmas Carols. Sitting there in the cottage, Christian even sang a bit of it, to Maggie's enjoyment. The time he spent with them always stood out as happy times.

Maggie spoke about the time she was leaving church after choir practice and she found a kitten hiding by the outside basement steps of the church. There was a group of neighborhood children that had cornered the scared little animal and they were throwing snowballs at it. Maggie, who was usually very shy, charged over to those little bullies and ran them off. She sat with the shivering kitten in her jacket trying to warm it until her mom drove up to take them home. There was a little gleam in Maggie's eyes as she recounted the story. They continued to share stories back and forth and it made them both feel a million times better. Maggie and Christian were really enjoying getting to know each other better. In that moment, it was just as if they were the only two people in the world.

After dinner was finished though, she wanted to bring up how she felt and finally thought of a way to do it, by connecting the story he had told her earlier that year. The heartfelt story of how the local loch had received its name, Loch Grádh. "Do you believe in the kind of love that was shared between Sir Aylwin and Denalla?" She quietly asked.

Christian didn't say anything at first and Maggie thought she may have frightened him with her question. The music we in between songs and the moment of silence seemed to last an eternity. She learned she was wrong with that assumption when he finally answered.

"I do Maggie." This was actually a subject that was very close to his own heart, so he made sure to think through what he wanted to say before he answered. "I am a romantic and I know that these days that is a rare thing."

"I know. It is difficult to find a good match with someone who understands love, true love, from the heart." She paused, then, before he could say anything else, Maggie continued, "I believe you are that type of person."

They had touched on the subject before and he wasn't sure where she was directing the conversation. When she didn't continue with her last statement, he started to clarify what he was saying. Maggie abruptly cut him off because she really wanted to finish what she had finally built up the courage to say to him. "Christian, I believe you have a good heart and that if you just allowed yourself to love, you would make someone, the right woman, the happiest person in the world."

"Maggie that is very sweet of you..."

She still wouldn't let him finish. Maggie was determined to finally say what she had on her mind. She had praying to Jesus prior to starting this conversation and for days prior. As she was speaking, she finally felt a courage that she had never felt before.

"I know that I have my struggles but so do you." She was not being condescending as she said this. She was only stating a valid point. "I know that one of yours is the inability to open your heart more than just a crack. I also know, from what little I have been able to see of it, it is so full of love and wanting to be loved, that it is a deeper struggle than some of the things I go through."

The aroma from the dinner still lingered in the cottage. Still sitting at the dining room table, Christian sat quietly across from her as she opened up more than she had ever done before. This time it wasn't about her. It was her observations about him. This was something that he wasn't used to. He rarely got close enough to anyone for them to even see that side of him. Maggie on the other hand was able to see it based on her own efforts, even when he tried to hide it. She spent the next fifteen minutes explaining to him what she thought true love should be like.

"You are a good man and I really want to see what can happen when we both let down our walls and allow love to enter in." She had said what she wanted to say now it was his turn to open up and say what he thought. She had shut him down a few times when he tried to talk a bit ago.

Christian sat in silence for a few moments. He was taking long enough for Maggie to think that she had made a big mistake telling him the things she did. In the end, she knew that no matter what he said or didn't say, she did the right thing.

"Maggie, while we were at the castle, I told you that I was falling in love with you."

Now it was her turn to start to interrupt him but he cleared his throat to signal that he wanted to finish. As she moved from the kitchen to the sofa in the living room, she smile and nodded, knowing that he was politely telling her that he wanted to finish. Christian followed her and sat in the chair near her.

"You are a wonderful woman that has more strength than anyone that I have ever known before. You came to a foreign country where you did not know a soul. You walked into a pub and became friends with someone that you never knew before that day. There is so much more to you than you have ever given yourself credit for. That is the beauty that is inside of you that people are drawn to, including me Maggie."

Maggie was getting very uncomfortable with all the

compliments and the fact the he was able to see right through her. It wasn't that what he was saying was wrong, she just didn't want to hear these things that bared her soul. She was also a little taken back because he hadn't commented on what she had said.

"I spend all my time not with you, wanting to be with you. The time that I am with you, I can't imagine being anywhere else." There it was. He responded, not with empty words, but by giving her examples of his actions. He hoped she understood what he was trying to say.

That was all she was gonna allow him to say. What little he did say meant more to her than anything he could have clouded the moment with. He stood up and sat next to her on the sofa. She placed her head on his shoulder, he placed his arm around hers, and they stayed like that until they both fell asleep. A short time later, she got up and went to bed, leaving him to sleep on the sofa covered up by her favorite blanket that she had brought with her from America.

~~~~~~~~~~~~

The next two weeks, went by in a bit of a flash. They spent all their time together when he wasn't working, just enjoying each other's company. It didn't matter what they were doing, whether it was her putting the finishing touches on her thesis or just sitting watching television. All that mattered to either of them was that they were together.

That was important because one day they were together when Maggie had begun complaining of abdominal pain. They were sitting in the living room of her cottage talking about her thesis when she doubled over. Christian jumped out of the chair that he had been sitting in and by the time he took the two steps over to the sofa where Maggie was sitting, he knew there was trouble. Without allowing her to contest his actions, he immediately got her into the car and raced her to the ER.

CHAPTER TWENTY-THREE

Less than a week later, Christian was in the kitchen waiting for Maggie to call. They were planning on meeting at his place and then go for a drive out in the country. It was something he used to do when he was back in the US and had done a few times with Maggie. He knew that her evening in the emergency room had really taken its toll on her. The ER doctor wanted to admit her but, after a discussion between the two of them, the doctor finally decided to sign discharge papers with a promise from the young American that she would get some rest and try to heal. Christian thought that getting out and seeing the countryside would do her some good. He knew the Maggie wasn't happy if she felt confined anywhere and they planned that the next day they would do the little road trip. She was supposed to be at his flat by 9:00am. It was now past 10:30 and he still hadn't heard from her. Christian was growing very concerned as it was very unlike Maggie to be this late.

He was not the type of person to show up at someone's house unannounced but something deep inside was telling him to go over to her house and check on her. The last seven days had been stressful as she was trying to heal from her trip to the emergency room. Today was causing even more stress because the few phone calls he made to her had gone unanswered. That in itself wasn't the concern because when she didn't answer, she would at least call back in a few minutes. The concern was that since his first call earlier that morning, he still had not received a call back. Christian had been in the medical field long enough that he knew to trust his instincts and the red flags when they were present. He decided that he could no longer wait for that call from Maggie and headed out to her cottage.

He arrived at her place less than ten minutes later. The red flags were in full gear as he walked up the sidewalk that lead to her front door. There was nothing out of the ordinary. Her rented car was in the driveway. The door was closed. There was a light coming from the living room window. Everything seemed to be in order. However, there was something though that he could not shake. He did everything he could to not race to the door. If she was ok, he didn't want to alarm her by rushing up and pounding on the door but there was something that kept telling him to hurry. He said a quick prayer asking God to be with her.

From the outside, nothing looked wrong with what he was looking at but still something was urging him to hurry and get inside. His instincts were pushing him each step of the way. When he finally reached the door, he knocked and waited for what seemed like a lifetime for her to answer. Although it had really only been less than a minute, he just couldn't wait any longer for her to answer. His instincts were now shouting at him to stop stalling and get inside. He decided to stop being polite. He reached for the door handle and said her name as he walked through the unlocked door.

All his medical training and experience didn't prepare him for what he saw when he pushed the door open. Just on the other side of the door, his heart broke as he took in the scene. His experience taught him to take in everything at once and do an assessment in order to proceed with what needed to be done. In an emergent situation one had to do this quickly and accurately. That is what made him good at his job. This was different. This was someone that he loved. As his heart was breaking, he prayed again to Jesus that she was going to be ok.

Maggie was lying on the sofa against a couple of big pillows. She had the red velvet blanket he had given her for Christmas on top of her with only her head and the top of her shoulders visible. After a quick assessment, he found that there was a gentle rise to her chest and he finally knew that she was breathing. He let out a sigh and finished his visual assessment before he walked over to wake her. The one thing that concerned him was the droplets of blood that had been running from the corner of her mouth down the pillow and onto the floor. It was drying but still very evident that it was fresh.

Christian called for a rescue squad. After hanging up with the dispatcher, he woke her so he could make sure that she was stable. He also wanted to make sure that she wasn't alarmed when EMS arrived and started to do their work up on her. He had been able to wake her long enough to tell her the plan. After just a few minutes, she had fallen right back asleep. Maggie stirred only once when the rescue workers were getting her set for transport. The police were also present and asking questions so they could understand what exactly had happened. Christian knew most of the first responders, so he knew the questions were procedural just making sure that there was no foul play. He answered them as he watched all the commotion, trying to stay focused with what the police were asking but his concern was growing more and more. Moments later, the police made a statement that they were confident that there was no foul play. The EMTS secured Maggie on the stretcher and then rolled her to the back of the ambulance. Once secured, Christian sat on the bench next to this woman that he loved. The driver raced around to the front and in seconds they were moving towards the hospital with the sirens blaring and Christian's heart breaking.

~~~~~~~~~~~~

Maggie had finally stabilized after arriving in the hospital. Three days later, she was set to be discharged from the hospital, with the doctor strongly advising her to stop the drinking. Her liver, which had been an ongoing issue, was barely hanging on. The bleeding issue was from her esophagus and stomach that had ulcers due to her bulimia. The eating disorder not only messed with her weight, it was causing issues throughout her entire system by not allowing any vitamins and nutrients from all the healthy food that she did eat to be absorbed into her body. The resulting problem was that the healing that should have been happening wasn't taking place. Christian knelt next to her bed as she was taking a nap awaiting her discharge instructions from the physician and her nurse.

Quietly he prayed, "Heavenly Father, this is one of your children. I believe that You brought her into my life so that we could teach each other to grow in You. You are a God of grace and mercy and I have seen You work many times in the lives of the people that have come through these doors. I am asking that You, my Gracious God, would watch over this beautiful soul of a woman and heal her. I believe that she has so much to accomplish for Your kingdom." Maggie stirred ever so slightly causing Christian to be distracted for a moment. Once she was settled again, he continued his prayer. "Thank you Heavenly Father for the time that You have given me to spend with Maggie. I pray that You heal her. I ask for Your forgiveness of our sins and no matter what happens, I pray that You will guide us in Your ways. In Jesus' name I pray, Amen."

He sat for a brief moment before getting back to his feet. Heading to the cafeteria for a quick bite, Christian was about to leave Maggie's room, when her nurse, walked in with the discharge paperwork. He woke her to let her know it was time to leave. After her nurse left the room, Maggie slowly got up to get dressed while Christian walked out ahead and pulled his car around to the front of the hospital. As he was opening the door to get out and go in and gets this lovely woman from her hospital room, her nurse was already bringing her out in a wheelchair. Maggie looked very weak and pale. She offered a faint smile and Christian was happy to see it and returned the smile, hoping that she wasn't able to detect the concern on his face. Once she was secure in the front seat of his car, the helpful RN placed a gentle, comforting hand on his shoulder and wished Maggie the best of luck.

Over the next week, Maggie was starting to stabilize even more and she was almost to the point of her being back to her normal self. Christian had received permission from his supervisor to take some time off and help get his friend healthy. A couple of days after she was discharged, Christian informed Maggie that he had spoken with her parents and that everyone agreed that she needs to go back home to Ohio.

"You have got to be kidding me. You are going to send me home when things get bad?" She was very upset when he first brought the subject to her. "I thought you really cared about me. Why would you send me away?" Maggie was crying and her emotions were getting the best of her. It was evident that she thought he was abandoning her.

"Maggie," Christian was talking softly trying not to get upset himself and further ignite the stressful situation. "Maggie, I am not sending you away. I care about you more than you can ever imagine."

"Then why are you sending me back to Ohio?" She was able to control her crying for a moment, as she waited for his answer.

"I am not sending you back. I am taking you there myself." Christian was starting to get emotional himself. He had confirmed that he was able to take an indefinite amount of time to take her back to the United States. "I will stay there as long as it takes for you to get healthy and then we can come back here if you would like that."

Maggie dried the few tears that were remaining in the corner of her eyes. She had stopped crying when he told her his plan and started to smile. Once she realized his intentions and that he would be there every step of the way, she realized just how much he cared for her. Maggie then agreed that it was best for her to go back home to be with her parents as she recuperated. Maggie finally agreed to it, with one other condition, that they could have dinner one more time at The Pipers. He agreed and later that night they went and shared a meal. Well Christian ate a little and Maggie barely touched her food. He knew that even though she wanted him to believe she was doing great, she wasn't quite up to par yet. He did know that that particular dinner was not about the meal as much as it was about the memory of the times that they had shared there.

While they sat and enjoyed their time there together, Angus made his way over and actually sat down with the two of them. This was completely out of character for him. Christian believed that it was because he had heard that Maggie had been in the hospital. He had only sat with the American couple for a few minutes before he got back up to tend to his other customers but the effect had been made on Maggie and it really cheered her up. The concerned Scotsman walked away from the table only after making the young lass promise that she would return. It made her feel good that he cared enough to sit there and want them to return. The couple were planning on leaving in a couple of weeks so Maggie agreed that she would return, if not before leaving for American, she would return once they arrived back in Scotland. Angus agreed and walked away, but not before giving Christian a knowing look.

CHAPTER TWENTY-FOUR

Two days later, Maggie's health started to deteriorate again. At first, he was not sure just how serious it was but, after a couple days, what should have been obvious from the beginning finally dawned on Christian. Maggie was in serious danger. Christian finally thought that it would be best that her parents would be there with her. So without her knowing, he finally called them and helped arrange for them to come for a visit.

Maggie's parents were expecting them to be back in the United States in less than two weeks and Christian surely didn't want to alarm them too much when he called to let them know what was happening with their daughter. She didn't want him to make the call because she insisted it was nothing more than being exhausted and if the doctors would just let her go back to her cottage, she would be fine after a few days of much needed sleep. What Maggie seemed to keep forgetting, was that he worked in medicine. He knew how to read a chart. She had put Christian on her privacy notice which gave the doctors permission to discuss her health and health care with him. What her doctors told him caused great concern in Christian and he knew he had to let her parents know. He knew this wasn't how they wanted to spend the first couple of weeks of the new year.

Mr. and Mrs. Greene's visit to Scotland was over four months ago. While they were there, he had developed a good rapport with them. He had spoken to them quite a few times since they left so when Maggie got sick it wasn't uncomfortable at all to be calling them. There was something, however that was making him nervous and that was the reason for the call. He had made this type of call before. In the past though, it was to family members he didn't know of patients he had never met prior to them arriving in the EC of the Royal Infirmary of Loch Grádh. Christian was a compassionate man, even though to look at him, most people's first thought of him was that he was intimidating. Christian could understand this thought of him because the wall he kept up helped him to keep his heart protected and out of danger of hurt and pain. This approach also helped him in his job as a nurse. However, the best part of his personality that made him good at his job was that he was kind and compassionate when he needed to be.

The first call he had made was difficult, but this one was even more so. This time she was sliding downhill faster. Now, sitting on the phone listening to the ringing, waiting for someone on the other end in Toledo, Ohio USA to answer, he was trying to gain the courage to be able to tell Maggie's parents that their daughter was in the hospital well over 3500 miles from where they were.

"Mrs. Greene, this is Christian Emerson," he said as she answered her phone with a smile. He had given them his number while they were visiting. As they departed back to the US, they had told him to keep their number and if he needed them for anything he would always be welcome to call. Christian was enjoying getting to know them and was happy every time they did talk, until that day. Now this woman that he cared about and loved was in the hospital again due to vomiting blood and complaining of abdominal pain.

"Hi Christian, how is everything going with you?" Mrs. Greene seemed happy to hear from him. Then she added, "How is Maggie?" Her motherly intuition hit and she knew that something was wrong.

He paused, not knowing how to continue. On the job, when he had to make this kind of call, he was compassionate but he dealt in facts. His patients and their family members appreciated that type of approach. Christian believed that if he laid out the facts as best as he could, the patients and the families could make a better decision on what path they should take towards their healing. He had found that they never wanted incoherent babble by medical professionals that were too afraid to be direct.

This call however, was very different. He was on the phone with someone he knew and held in high respect. Even more, this was the mother of someone he cared very deeply for, someone he loved more than he ever thought he would allow himself to love anyone.

"Mrs. Greene, is Mr. Greene there with you?" He asked

quietly. She sensed that what he was about to say was very important and from how Christian was acting it didn't seem good. She answered his question by taking the phone away from her mouth and hollering to another room for Nelson to pick up the extension next to where he was working.

"Hello." Christian immediately recognized the voice of Maggie's father.

"Hello Mr. Greene."

"Well hello, Christian. How is everything?" He asked in a quiet yet very concerned voice. Mr. Greene wanted his daughter home so that he knew what was happening with her. "Are you two getting packed and ready to come back?"

"Well to be honest," he said, speaking to both of them, "not so well." Not mentioning anything about the preparations to come back.

There was silence on the other end of the line for what seemed like a lifetime. He was beginning to think he had lost the connection when Mrs. Greene spoke up.

"What happened? Is Maggie okay?" He could tell by the solemn tone in her voice that this was a call that they were not surprised to get, especially with how bad Maggie had been feeling the second to last day of their trip to visit her in Scotland.

He took an audibly deep breath before he started to explain to them what had happened over the last few hours. As he started to explain, his instinct kicked in and started to explain in clinical terminology.

"Maggie is back in the hospital where I work. When she first arrived, she was immediately ushered back to my section. My coworkers know her and knew that I would be the one to take care of her. I did an assessment and found that her chief complaint was esophageal bleeding and mid to upper abdominal pain. Upon further assessment, she admitted to waking up the last two mornings coughing up blood."

He paused, waiting to see if they had any questions. When neither of them said anything, he asked if they were still there. After both had answered yes, he continued.

"We took some blood from her and the lab ran all the tests they could. I consulted with the doctor on duty and came to the conclusion that she has cirrhosis of the liver due to increased consumption of alcohol. The diagnosis was also confirmed with an ultrasound of her liver. This is a big issue because if she doesn't stop drinking, her liver will fail and she will not recover." He wanted to explain the situation in more detail but he could tell by their response that they understood what he was saying. There was also more to the diagnosis and after giving them a moment for what Christian told them already to sink in, he went on to explain. Just as he was about to speak, Mrs. Green had a question.

"Is there anything else that we should know?" Her parents wanted to know all the information before they reacted. Christian was impressed with how they were taking the news. He knew that most would have thought it was cold how he was informing Mr. and Mrs. Greene. Christian knew from the time he spent with them that they preferred this information directly.

"As you know, the eating disorder she is suffering with is destroying her as well. Part of the reason her liver is in bad shape is because the lack of nutrition to regenerate her body. The seriousness of this is compounded with the two issues combined."

Maggie's parents took in what he was saying and they were very thankful that he was there with their daughter.

Finally Mrs. Greene asked, "In your experience, and from what you can tell from the scans and discussing this with her doctor, is there any chance that she will heal?" Christian was impressed with her straight forwardness. He didn't want to hide anything from them.

"In my experience," he just couldn't finish the sentence. Christian took a deep breath but choked before he could say anything. Finally he was able to answer her question, which was the same thing he asked Maggie's doctor not fifteen minutes earlier. "No. I do not believe that she will be able to overcome this."

Again, he paused waiting to see if there were any questions. This time he didn't ask if they were still there, he needed to continue in order to get through everything that needed to be said. He was breaking down. He just told his girlfriend's parents that she may not overcome her sickness and there was still a little more to be said.

"The last bit of news, her doctors are asking for you to come out here and help with her care. Even though they know that she and I are together, they need the closest family members to be here to help determine what you want done." Christian had finished what he needed to say and then sat in silence while he waited for them to say something.

Her mom finally spoke up saying that they both thought they knew of the eating disorder since she had been under a doctor's care back in Toledo, trying to help her overcome that issue. The alcohol issue was something that they had suspected but they hadn't been completely sure of, not until that moment, that is.

Christian went on to explain her behavior almost since the day they had met. He mentioned that he noticed she would order a diet soda when they were at The Pipers but then every once in awhile she would reach into her purse and take a drink of her diet soda from a bottle she kept stored in there. He had thought the behavior odd but at first let it pass. He thought that maybe she preferred the bottled version because it tasted more like what she was used to back in the US. The soda that is served in restaurants over in the UK tasted different. Christian knew that from his experience when he first moved there.

He went on to explain to Mr. Greene that they had discussed the subject but a few times she got very defensive so they didn't get far. So at that time, he let the subject go. Her parents were still listening intently to what he was saying. He let that info sink in with them.

Mrs. Greene was the one to finally break the brief silence. "What is it that we are looking at? What do you mean 'her liver is failing'?"

It was at that moment that Christian really started to breakdown. He had been trying to keep his composure, tried to stay in his professional mind frame. He knew he had to give a straightforward answer because that is how Mr. Greene preferred answers to his direct questions.

"Mr. Greene," Christian couldn't say anything else for a moment. He stopped and took a deep breath.

"Go ahead, son. We can handle this."

Christian was surprised at the tenderness in his voice. He was again impressed with the genuine love this family shared between each other. It was something Christian had no experience with but was glad they was there for Maggie. He took another deep breath as his charge nurse, who had just sat down to add her support, leaned over and placed a gentle hand on Christian's shoulder. Feeling a little better, he nodded to her, then into the phone started to explain what was happening with Margaret Elizabeth Greene.

~~~~~~~~~~

"As soon as she is stable, I would like her to come home immediately. I don't want you to wait for the flight you guys have already booked. I will have two new tickets for you both at the ticket desk by tomorrow. I want you to bring her home." Mr. Greene told Christian. He was very direct in his statement to the younger man. There was no anger. There was only the concern of a father that was unable to be near his daughter to take care of her and keep her safe.

Christian had no children of his own but he understood the concern that Mr. Greene had. He was just as worried about Maggie. He also felt helpless. All his training and experience was useless because there was nothing he could do to help her. Mrs. Greene sat quietly listening to the two of them talking. Her heart was breaking and she wasn't sure what to say or what to do. In the end, the only thing she wanted was to have her oldest daughter back home.

"I will make sure that happens. I will also keep you updated on her progress." All three hung up and Mr. Greene had seemed content with where things were left at that moment.

Christian made sure the call had ended and then locked the screen on his cell phone. After placing it into his pocket he walked back into Maggie's room. She was awake but she was looking very pale. When he said her name, she very slowly turned in his direction and gave him a faint smile. Christian knew her smiles well and it was obvious to him that that smile was forced.

"Maggie?" Christian spoke quietly. She had been asleep

for almost twelve hours.

"Hi," she replied in a whisper that was almost too soft for him to hear. "Can we go home now?"

CHAPTER TWENTY-FIVE

In the grand scheme of life, Christian hadn't known Maggie Greene for that long of time, but they experienced more in that short time than he had with just about anyone he had ever known. She breezed into his life, dusted out the cobwebs in his heart, and taught him how to live and love again. He knew that no matter how long or how short his days were here on earth, he knew that Maggie would always have a place in his heart. It wasn't until a couple of weeks later that he realized just how much of an effect she had in his life. It was because of their time together and everything that had happened that he went back to the US to be with her while she was in the hospital.

He had taken an extended leave from the Royal

Infirmary he had been working at in Scotland. He decided to stay in the United States indefinitely. He knew he would be there for his dear Maggie Greene. I still can't believe she is struggling like this, he thought. He never really thought he would have come back here to this side of The Pond but there was no way in the world he could have stayed away. This woman meant too much to him. His plan was to only be there for a few days and then head back to his life in Scotland, with Maggie. Mr. Greene had other ideas.

Christian was standing in the ICU room at Master Memorial Medical Center in the western side of Toledo, Ohio. Maggie's family was all in the room with him as they stood watching over her. Maggie's doctor in Toledo had put her in an induced coma to help slow down the destruction that was tearing at her body. It was a sad scene. Eliza was sitting in a chair, next to her bed, painting Maggie's finger nails. Her mom was sitting in another chair, right behind her youngest daughter, watching both of them together. Uncle Fred was standing next to Eliza's husband, Howard, at the foot of the bed. Nelson was standing next to Christian. In the back ground was the faint beep of the machines that were monitoring Maggie's vitals. The nurse came in, wrote down a few numbers that she needed for her charting and quietly left the room.

"What can you tell us from her vitals?" Mr. Greene quietly asked Christian.

"All I can say is that it doesn't look good." Christian couldn't tell them anything more than what the nurse watching over her had already told them. He knew they wanted more answers, hopeful answers but at that point there was nothing he could say. So he prayed a silent prayer with everyone in the room. Heavenly Father, we are all gathered here to watch over our beloved Maggie. Please be with her and heal her. Take away her pain and bring her back to us. In Jesus' name I pray. Amen.

~~~~~~~~~~

Christian had closed his eyes for a moment trying to fight back the tears. He couldn't believe what was happening. When he opened his eyes, he watched as the family was standing close to each other, hugs being passed between them. Eliza looked over her dad's shoulder at Christian and walked over and gave him a hug. Christian pulled her mom and dad into the hug. They followed suit with the rest of the family and in a moment, everyone in the room was standing together in another hug that had more love in it than Christian had ever felt in his in entire life. He had never seen a family care about each other as much as this family was showing right then.

None of them knew how long they stood like that. It wasn't until Maggie's nurse Jenn came into the room to check on her again that the rest of the family broke the hug and went back to what they were doing. They were quiet as Jenn moved about the room. The nurse wrote down the vitals off the machine hanging from the wall near Maggie's hospital bed. It was part of her regular routine and she was in hourly to do it. She then excused the family from the room so she could clean and wash Maggie and then changed her bedding.

Christian looked at Mr. Greene who nodded in return. Christian then turned to Jenn and stated that he would stay in the room and give her a hand. Jenn accepted his offer and closed the door as the last family member left the room. The two nurses had worked together in the past in the emergency room at the hospital on the other side of Toledo.

Once alone, Christian asked Jenn a few questions about what the doctor's plan of care for Maggie was.

"They are at a loss. They know that her liver is failing and that is what is causing all the distention in her abdomen." She was talking about the changes in her condition since she arrived back into the States.

"How far gone is her liver? Is there any chance to stabilize the decline?"

"Her liver isn't the worst part. You know she also suffers with an eating disorder, don't you?"

"Yes," he replied thinking back to all the times they had eaten a meal together and Maggie had immediately gone to the restroom right after. She would say she was going to brush her teeth, so he had never thought much of it beyond that. Eventually though, he realized the truth and then she explained the disorder to him when they were sitting together in the cafeteria at the Royal Infirmary where he worked. He remembered the sadness he felt that day when she opened up and told him about her struggles. His training kept him always on his toes. So he had spent every day since then trying to figure out what the underlying issue was. If that could've been dealt with maybe she wouldn't be in the situation. In this he felt that he failed her as a loved one.

"Well the eating disorder has done more damage to her system than the alcohol consumption. Because she never let anything settle in her system, no nutrients were allowed to regenerate damaged cells." Jenn was speaking in a professional manner trying to communicate in a way that was compassionate but not too emotional. She was not succeeding. She had taken care of Maggie on a previous visit and really liked her. She had chosen to take care of her again when Maggie arrived in the ICU three days prior.

Christian was on autopilot as he held the sheets up so Jenn could give Maggie a quick sponge bath. When she was finished, he helped Jenn change the sheets out from underneath his dear sweet friend that now laid in an induced coma, as she struggled to hang onto life.

"On top of all that she is struggling with because of the eating disorder and her failing liver, she now has pneumonia and that is actually a growing concern right now. The doctor is saying that if they cannot get that under control..." Jenn couldn't finish her statement. She was kind hearted and good at her job but she just couldn't bring herself to finish. Christian knew what the nurse was trying to say even though she couldn't get the words out. He also knew the family would come back in here and want to know what he found out. How does someone tell a family that has accepted him like this family has, that their daughter will probably not make it? His training never prepared him for this. His experience was all but useless at that very moment.

Christian was watching her breathing. Maggie's breaths were now coming in slow and shallow. The familiar beep of the heart monitor was keeping silent rhythm in the background as Mr. and Mrs. Green walked back in the room after taking a break out in the hallway for about an hour. Christian had given them an update on what the nurse had said during her last rounding. Christian had barely left the side of this woman his heart was breaking over. Maggie was still in the Intensive Care unit at Master Memorial Medical Center in northwest Ohio and at this point she was struggling to hold on to her life.

Christian was exchanging glances from the heart

monitor and watching her chest slowly rise. Over the last couple of months the two of them had been in this position a few times and Christian spent a lot of his time in silent prayer, asking Jesus to take away her pain and heal her. The room was silent with the exception of the monitor as Eliza and her husband walked into the room. There was an IV drip running trying to keep Maggie hydrated. No one was saying anything. It was as if they knew what was coming. Christian glanced at Maggie's chest and the rhythm was slowing. He knew her family was in the room with him, but now he was vaguely aware of them or anything else around him. His eyes were transfixed on Maggie and he knew in his heart that this was the end. The heart monitor alerted that her heartbeat was slowing. Brian was the nurse on shift and he walked in to check. He looked over at Christian. Christian was still staring at Maggie. Brian made an adjustment to her IV drip and the monitor stopped the alert. After a moment her vitals stabilized.

~~~~~~~~~~

Christian walked out of the room after they had finished.

"Let's go to the cafeteria and grab something to eat." The family had been in the room for hours watching over Maggie. No one was sure how long it had been since any of them had eaten.

Mr. Greene was the first one to speak up. "He's right. We all need to get a bite to eat."

While they all sat in the cafeteria, they made small talk trying to not think about what was happening just down the hall. Christian sat quietly, listening to the family talk. He was so deep in his own thoughts that he didn't hear when Eliza asked him how he and Maggie had met.

CHAPTER TWENTY-SIX

When they arrived back at Maggie's room less than thirty minutes later, the doctor came in and spoke to the family. His update wasn't good. He told them that there was nothing else they could do. The time had come for them to make a very difficult choice. Up until that point, a major part of Christian was in professional mode. He had been in similar situations before and had been able to handle it. This was different, now that it had come down to this very moment. Now he didn't want to have to help make this decision. Maggie's family was strong. There was a lot of love in this room watching over Maggie. Christian did what he thought best, he closed his eyes and silently prayed. Heavenly Father, there is a lot of pain in this room. There is also a lot of love. Love I believe You put here. It is not something I am used to but I know it is from You. Please help them. Be with them. Help them to make the right decision on what to do. I also pray that Maggie is in Your hands. In Jesus' name I pray, Amen.

After the doctor left the room, not a word was spoken. Mr. Greene looked around the room and gave a nod to Christian. The younger man walked out of the room so the family could discuss what they were planning to do. Earlier in the cafeteria, Nelson discussed with Christian that he wanted him to be a part of the decision. However, the brave father had told Christian that he once they received a few questions answered by the doctor, those answer would determine what the final decision of the family would be.

Christian sat on a bench in the hallway just outside of Maggie's room. He was silently crying as his heart was being torn to shreds in his chest. He never thought that they would be in this position. He never thought that he would ever have to say goodbye to her, especially like this. Time stopped moving as he waited for Mr. Greene to give him the ok to come back into the room. All the memories from ever moment that Maggie and Christian spent together went through his head. Love for her was filling his heart and breaking it at the same time.

When he walked back in the room Christian looked at Mr. Green and slowly shook his head. No one else in the room noticed that interaction. Although no words were spoken, the communication between the two men was clear. Mr. Greene then told Christian the family had made while he was getting confirmation from the doctor on the treatment plan.

Mr. Greene informed him that they had made their

decision and that they were going to pull life support. The family stood around Maggie's bed. Eliza asked Christian to say a prayer. They all stood each with a hand on Maggie, each wanting to have that physical connection with her. Then she took her last breath. It was over. She was gone. No words were spoken, well none that Christian could hear. He stood next to the bed, his eyes transfixed on Maggie's face. She looked so peaceful. Her thin lips were pressed together. Her eyelids closed and covered the depth that her grayish/green eyes hid.

He wasn't sure how long he had stood there like that. Mr. Greene, who had been standing barely five feet away brought him out of his trance when he placed a hand on Christian's shoulder. The younger man looked up at this kind man with tears in his eyes. He had known Maggie for over a year. They had spent so much time together in Scotland and she had become a regular part of his life. He couldn't believe that she was no longer here. A part of him was a little jealous because right at that moment, she was in the presence of Jesus. As happy as that thought made him, he was dying a little on the inside knowing that he wouldn't get to see her for a long time.

"Son," Mr. Greene had moved his hand from Christian's shoulder and had given him a hug.

Christian was caught off guard to hear Mr. Greene call him 'son'. With the poor relationship he had had with his father, he never thought he would hear that word directed at him again.

"Son," Mr. Greene repeated, "just because Maggie is no longer with us, we don't want you to stop calling and talking to us. Maggie thought very highly of you and we can see why. You are a good man and have been very supportive through all of this."

Christian was shocked to hear those words. He thought very highly of Mr. and Mrs. Greene and he could see where Maggie inherited all her good qualities. They were very unselfish people. This couple knew their daughter better than anyone. Christian had spent only a short time with her, but she had had a tremendous impact on his life. He had never wanted to return to the United States, yet here he was. After all the pain he had suffered in his life, he had sworn he would never let anyone into his heart again. Yet, Margaret Elizabeth Greene had made her way in without any effort at all. She was a good woman and after spending the time he had with her and her family, he could see where she got it from.

"Yes sir, Mr. Greene."

"One more thing, you can no longer call me that. Please, just call me Nelson."

"Ok," Christian paused, then added, "Nelson."

Maggie's father pulled Christian in and gave him another hug. Both men cried at the emptiness of her passing. The world felt dimmer without her in the room. No one in the room had to say anything but it was something felt by all in the room.

~~~~~~~~~~~

She's gone, he thought. The last two weeks with Maggie in the ICU went by without much realization on his part that time was passing. He vaguely remembered standing at her side as she lay in her hospital bed. There was a bustle of people coming in and out or her room, checking the monitors when they alarmed. The nurse would push a button on the machine and the alarm would stop. As she was fading, the alarm would alert again and again.

That was all before. Now he was standing alone in the room with her. The hospital staff was no longer coming in and out. Her family had said their goodbyes and they were waiting just outside of her room for him to come out. He just sat there in the chair next to her bed. Christian had given her a hug, whispering in her ear words she would never hear. He leaned in and gave her a kiss on her forehead a couple of times. Now he was just holding her hand and whispering another prayer giving thanks that Jesus had healed her. It wasn't the way that he had hoped but she was in His Presence which meant she was healed. So Christian knew that he had to give thanks.

True love isn't about feelings. It is about sacrifice. God showed us how much He loves us by sacrificing His only Son for us. What have we done to deserve such a love? Absolutely nothing. This love was given freely. Not only have we done nothing to earn this love, we have gone to the opposite end of the scale and we do things that should make it so we never receive it. However, God doesn't love us on our terms. He loves us on His terms. He teaches us to love others in the same way He loves us. We fail at this because we are failing human beings. We are, however, commanded to try by Jesus Himself.

Love honestly.

Love unselfishly.

Love unconditionally.

Love knowing you may lose everything.

Love with all your heart, through the smiles and the pain that life can bring.

CHAPTER TWENTY-SEVEN

Nelson and Connie invited Christian to join them as they made the funeral arrangements two days later. Christian, who was still in shock at her passing, accepted their invitation to help. They were sitting at the funeral home picking out a casket and the rest of the details that went with funeral arrangements. They were doing their best to get through this meeting. A lot of memories were shared while they sat and picked out the outfit she would be buried in, what color casket, what music would be played, the memorial video of pictures, and more. Christian had no experience in this part, so his contributions were few. He was however, very glad that he would be there to help and listen to Mr. and Mrs. Greene and their remaining daughter share their favorite moments.

Maggie's family had welcomed him in and he had never felt more at home than he did when he was in their company. Having been the last person to spend as much time with her as he had, they were thankful for his contributions. He had learned that Maggie had begun to push her friends away over the last few years. She had started her downward slide and she didn't want anyone to see it and think less of her. Christian did understand her thought process. Her trip to Scotland had awakened something in her that her family was overjoyed to see. They were shocked that she had decided to go and even more so when she extended her stay. They knew it was all because of him and they were happy he had a part in making her happy in the last part of her life.

Christian had learned that Maggie had sent multiple emails, letters and pictures to Eliza and her parents, going on and on about what a wonderful trip she had been having. They were surprised when she told them she was extending the trip from the planned two months for her research to an indefinite amount of time. That was what prompted her parents to come out and visit. Once they were there, they saw for themselves, that not only was she healthy, she was happier than they had seen her in a long time.

He sat and listened as her mom recalled memories of the trip, while the family gathered around the table in the conference room at the funeral home. He was on autopilot so his additions to the conversation were minimal.

~~~~~~~~~~~

She's gone. His heart was broken. Christian was in shock. He had spoken with her dad while they were at the hospital.

He had told Mr. Greene that he was looking forward to going back to Scotland. He wanted to be back where Maggie and he had shared so much time together. Mr. Greene understood what Christian was saying but he also wanted the younger man to know that no matter where he went, he would always have a family with them and that he should never stop being in contact with them.

Christian was caught off guard that day and with everything that had happened over the span of those four days when Maggie had passed away and then the funeral arrangements and then her burial. He was in shock and he knew that her family was feeling her loss much more than he was.

It had been two months since she passed away. His life had become nothing more than routine set on autopilot. He had contacted his supervisor back in Scotland and was given permission to take three months off. He had built up enough vacation time that he was able to stay in northwest Ohio without having to worry about losing his job. Not only did he have the time off, the Infirmary that he worked at in Scotland had an excellent bereavement plan for those that have lost a loved one. He was thankful to God for giving him such a wonderful employer, one that was as understanding as the one he had.

His life was nothing more than routine and the routine didn't comprise of much. They knew each other over a year and she was more imbedded in his heart than he ever could have imagined.

"How are things going for you?" Trista asked as she and Christian sat in the local coffee house together. Trista was an old friend that had moved from the Detroit area down to Toledo about five years ago. They had stayed in touch every so often over that time. When he arrived back in the United States she was the first and only person he called to share that Maggie was sick and when she passed away there was no one else that he could imagine talking to. Trista was nice enough to visit at the funeral home for the visitation and then the next day for the funeral service.

Now they were sitting at a local coffee house in the western side of Toledo, each with a warm drink sitting in front of them. Trista had taken a few sips of her drink but Christian's drink was cooling down and he hadn't even taken one sip yet.

"It's not about me. It is about her family and the loss they are struggling through." He was sincere in his comment but also wanted to turn the subject from him to the real situation at hand.

"I know but you also suffered a loss as well." She was referring to the many phone calls they had shared. Christian many times had called to vent to his closest friend. He knew what she was trying to do but he didn't want to talk about his feelings. He was used to shutting down when the pain of life became too unbearable and he had had more than his share of pain. Losing Maggie was at the top of the list and in that moment he didn't want face it. Trista on the other hand had other ideas. He was too numb to think but knew deep down that she was right. She had always been the voice of reason in times when his own logical mind was out of sorts.

"Tell me about her. Tell me some of the things that you two did while you were in Scotland." Trista was good at getting answers out of him on the rare times when he didn't want to face things head on. She was the only one in his life capable of such a feat.

"I remember the day we met as if it was yesterday. She

walked in The Pipers like a vision." He went on to explain the day they met and almost every minute of the times they shared together. She had heard this all before but sat quietly listening as he opened his heart and memory to all they shared.

When he was done, they sat there in silence for a few minutes. Christian finally took a sip of his coffee. By then it was ice cold. He didn't even notice as he took his second drink. That was the first time he had really faced his side of things. Christian cared very deeply for her family and tried to be a source of comfort for them. Unfortunately, he felt like all he was though, was a constant reminder to them of the loss they were struggling with.

After a few minutes, Trista finally spoke. "She was the love of your life."

Christian was in shock at what Trista had just said. He had never thought about his feelings. He had told Maggie that he loved her on many occasions. He was always worried about her. He knew he enjoyed spending time with her but he had kept his heart closed off because he thought if he ever opened up again, he would have to face the secrets he kept in the dark corners of his heart. He just looked at Trista unable to respond. He never thought about it like that before.

Trista could see that he was surprised by what she said so she gave him a few minutes to come to terms with what she had just dropped on him.

"What makes you say that?" was all he was able to say when he finally did speak.

"I have known you for years. I have never heard you talk about anyone the way you talk about Maggie."

The realization of her statement hit him like a ton of

bricks. Trista was right. Maggie was the love of his life. Part of him wished that Trista had not said anything. Knowing that her comment was true, there was now so much more regret that he had never realized just how he felt while Maggie was still alive, when he could have told her and shown her. The wall that he kept as a stronghold around his heart stopped him from living and truly loving. It stopped Christian from living a happy life filled with love, even if it was only destined for a short time.

It was knowledge that was good for him to realize. Yet why would his friend want to bring pain into his life? "Why would you say that?" He was really struggling with all the emotions coursing through his head and heart. Getting frustrated, "Why would you tell me that now?"

"I have known you a long time and I have never heard you talk like this about anyone." Trista was trying to understand what he was going through. How could someone feel that strong about someone and not even know it, she thought.

Neither of them really needed to answer that question. The answer was obvious. So they sat there for a little while longer making small talk. Trista knew that Christian didn't want to discuss the subject any further. He would need time to process that conversation.

She talked for about 20 minutes, knowing that Christian was zooming off with thoughts of his own. After a few minutes of silence, Christian had a request for his friend.

Trista knew that he would ask and said that she would be happy to.

~~~~~~~~~~~

Trista sat in her car as she waited for Christian. She

watched as he was standing at Maggie's grave site. The monument company did a great job on the design. Trista had learned from Christian that Maggie's favorite flower was a rose. Her family had a rose engraved into the stone right next to a picture of a cat, which was in memory of her favorite animal. Trista watched as Christian was talking. She wasn't able to hear but she knew him enough to have an idea of what he was saying. Trista could see the tears that were starting to fall as he spoke.

"I miss you Maggie. There are so many things I should have said to you while you were here. I'm sorry I let my own hurt and pain get in the way of you knowing just how much you mean to me. I didn't even know myself because of the pain of my own past." Tears were falling steadily now.

"You, walking into my life, was one of the best things that ever happened to me. I was surprised at how you made yourself at home in my heart from the minute we met. I don't expect that there will ever be a time when you will not be there." He felt like he was rambling but he knew he had to say these things, even though he knew she couldn't hear him. It was starting to make him feel better to finally admit what, until an hour ago, what he didn't fully know existed at the time he was with Maggie.

"I love you Maggie. I should have told you this a long time ago." Tears were still falling and he knew he couldn't control them, nor did he want to. He was finally letting the wall around his heart down. It was something that needed to happen a long time ago. Christian was letting his heart speak. "Maggie, I miss you and I love you."

~~~~~~~~~~

Christian and Trista left the cemetery after he had opened his heart. Maggie believed in Jesus as the Son of God so he knew that she was in heaven and that she hadn't heard a word he said. Christian did feel better about having said what should have been said while Maggie was still alive.

As Trista drove him to his car at the coffee house, he told her that he was nearing the end of his leave from the Infirmary. He had to make a decision on whether he was going back to Scotland or staying in the U.S. and giving up the job he enjoyed and worked so hard at.

"What do you think you are going to do? Which way are you leaning?" She asked with genuine concern in her voice and heart for her good friend.

"I don't know," he paused, and then added "If I stay here in Ohio, it will be nothing but pain. If I go back it will be to memories of Maggie." He didn't know what his answer was going to be. Finally he just said, "In truth, I just don't know."

Chapter Twenty-Eight

Angus was friendly enough as a business owner. He wasn't one to talk much as he was going about his business at the pub. As a matter of fact, Christian couldn't ever recall him stopping and having a conversation with anyone for longer than a few minutes. When that happened it was usually a customer that stopped him. Angus would give a fairly short answer and keep moving about doing the things he needed to do. He knew that the pub had been in Angus's family for a long time. Even though the pub owner was well known to the area, Christian didn't even remember seeing Angus about town. Almost everyone in the area knew his family, but the Scotsman was a bit of a mystery. Christian had learned, not long after arriving in Scotland, that even the locals could rarely get him to say anything. The American was usually good at getting people to talk. It was a trait that made him good at his job. However, there at The Pipers there was usually a lot of good conversation, except from Angus.

Christian was sitting at the pub waiting for Maggie to arrive. There were only two other patrons and they were both sitting at the bar. When Angus brought a glass of soda to where Christian was sitting, the American asked again about the piper in the area. He had asked the pub owner a few times over the past 12 months but like anyone he asked, he was met with resistance and had never received an answer.

Christian wasn't sure what was different about this day, but when he asked Angus again about the mysterious piper, he responded in a quiet voice and told him about what he wanted to know. Christian was caught off guard that he was going to answer, even more so when the middle aged Scotsman sat down at the table.

"Long before there were many people living in the area, even before the Stewarts lived in the castle, there was a family had been well known for the pipes they played." Christian knew part of the history but what he knew was mostly of the Stewarts and their part in the area.

"When Audric was placed here by the king of England, the nobleman hired this family to play when his knights were sent on to battle. It was this family member that was with Sir Aylwin when he was killed in battle. That same family member came back and told the nobleman the bad news. It was that same family member that played the pipes during the funeral. When Denalla threw the rose in the loch, he also played. As time went on, every time Denalla threw a rose into the loch, the piper played."

Christian sat and listened to the story the mysterious

pub owner was telling him. This was the longest conversation that the two of them had ever had. Angus was very in tune with his patrons and in that moment, he knew the struggles that Christian was suffering through with the loss of the woman that he had loved.

Angus finished his story and then left the American to his lunch and thoughts. He picked at his sandwich as he waited for Maggie to arrive. After an hour, a thought hit Christian like a ton of bricks. She isn't coming. She will never be here again. She is gone. Even though this knowledge wasn't something new, the thought caused his heart to break all over again. He wasn't losing his mind. Over the last year he had spent many days and evenings with Maggie sitting at this very table. It was instinct to be there. It was instinct to be expecting her to arrive but she was gone. She would never meet him there again.

CHAPTER TWENTY-NINE

On the banks of Loch Grádh, Christian was standing next to the bench where over the last year, he had spent many hours with Maggie talking about all kinds of things. He tossed a white rose into the dark water of the loch. As he stood there and watched the rose float away, a flood of emotions enveloped him and he was barely able to contain what was going through him. Part of him was frustrated that he ever opened his heart again. Had he just kept to himself, he wouldn't be feeling the pain of another lost love like he was going through at that moment.

However, if he had kept to himself, if he had never spoken up that day in The Pipers when that beautiful American woman was struggling to understand the Scottish owner of the pub, Christian would have not experienced one of the best years of his life. Even though it had only been just over a year, he was happy that he had the time with her that he did. Maggie had reached into his heart in a way that no one had ever been able to.

He was looking off across the water of the loch. The mist was rolling across the water that mid morning as he stood there. It was at that moment, he heard it again. The faint sound of bag pipes. He had never figured out where the piper was playing from but every time he heard it, it sent chills down his spine. Christian would sit with Maggie as they heard the piper when they were there together. That day, as he sat down on the bench next to the water, the flowers along the path starting to bloom, and the leaves on the tree growing and bringing green to the awakening landscape, the piper brought a haunting mystery to the surrounding area. Christian wasn't sure if it was wishful thinking but as he watched the water trickle up to the shore less than five feet from where he sat, the rose floated back to him. A flood of tears fell as he reached over to pick up the rose. In that moment, with the mysterious bag piper playing 'Amazing Grace', he realized that not only did he understand just how much he loved Maggie, he finally knew that she really did love him. Even though she was gone, his heart was full of love more than it had ever been. He stopped reaching toward the rose in the water. He backed his hand away and the wind changed direction and the rose floated back out toward the center of the loch. It was lost in the mist and Christian, still sitting said a quiet prayer of thanksgiving to Jesus.

When he stood up, a breeze coming down the side of the mountain lifted the mist just slightly. The colors of the landscape had a brightness that he couldn't remember ever seeing before. His eyes took in everything that surrounded him. Christian noticed the trees were dark brown, so much so that they almost looked black. The green of the leaves was so bright in contrast to the trunk and the branches, that if he hadn't known better, he would've guessed it was an artist rendition. The colors in the surrounding mountains poking through the top of the mist, was just as vibrant.

Christian had been down to the banks of Loch Grádh countless times over the last three years and the only thing that he could think of was that his tears were distorting the colors. It happened for only a brief moment when the mist had parted to reveal the piper. Christian felt like, well he couldn't help explain how he felt. As he stared at the water he wondered how many tears had fallen in to fill this loch over the years? How many silent prayers were prayed to God from broken hearts? The broken hearted man could only guess that the number was countless.

Christian looked off in the direction of the bagpiper. As the mist lifted, Christian was shocked to see the person standing on the eastern bank of the loch. The bagpiper gave him a slight nod. The mist which was still moving through the glen and across the water slowly enveloped the no longer mysterious person playing the timeless, yet haunting melody. When the figure was completely covered again, the song ended as the last few notes echoed through the valley.

-----*The End*-----

The Loch Grádh Legend
(Unedited xcerpt of Maggie's thesis paper)

~~The following is an excerpt of the thesis paper that Maggie was working on during the final year of her life. This portion contains the intro to her paper and part of The Legend of Loch Grádh. Had she been able to complete her paper, she would have received her MA in English and was planning to become and English teacher.~~

Love is a mystery for the ages. It is a story that is as old as time. Can it be told any differently? Is it so familiar that no one really wants to hear another one? Unlikely. Love stories tug at the heart. They make the reader feel like they are not alone in the world. No matter what story is told and no matter how familiar it can be, there is always someone who knows exactly what the character is going through, something to bring those two stories together.

Love comes in many forms. On one hand, we have the greatest expression and example of love from God. It was out of love that He created us. It was that same love that made Jesus come to earth. He was born to show us that God was still with us. He taught us many things. In Matt 22:37 he taught us that the greatest commandment is to love, "love the Lord your God with all your heart, with all your soul, and with all your mind." He went on to teach us to "love your neighbor as yourself." Straight from the mouth of our Savior is this commandment, the commandment that we should love.

In John 15:12-13, Jesus taught us, 'that you love one another as I have loved you. Greater love has no one than this, than to lay down one's life for his friends." Jesus was never one to just stand around and preach words. He would always allow His actions to back up His words. To prove this, He walked to the cross on His own accord. He suffered beatings, ridicule, and eventually death to pay the penalty for our sins. He did this for His friends, those that do whatever He commands us (John 15:14). The story of His love for us didn't end at the cross. It was evident in the empty tomb and in His resurrection. We will also see it fully in His glorious appearing when He returns. How many of us can say that we have ever loved anyone to the extent that we would die for them? How many of us would do it for someone that was beating us? My guess? Not many.

This kind of love has no equal. It is pure.

It is unconditional.

The best thing is this kind of love is a gift given freely

from God to those willing to accept it. Even though many have tried to duplicate this kind of love, it has never been equaled, nor could it ever be. However, because of its genuineness and purity, it never hurts to try.

Is this kind of love something that can be evident among each of us? I believe that love, genuine unconditional love is still around. It is most definitely rare, but it does exits. One such piece of evidence is actually something from my heritage. The story it is as follows:

Many, many years ago, the king of England was having trouble with the Scottish people, as it has been told to me by members of the family and what I could find in my research of local history, is it was in the late 14th century.

Many years ago, the king of England was having trouble with the Scottish people. The king wanted to have control over the whole island of Britain.

Despite his greed and desire to rule the whole island, the king was failing at the task because his castle was in the southern part of England. It was difficult to move supplies and an army the size he needed, that far away. It was also difficult because the people in the north didn't want to be ruled by a king that was as ruthless and greedy as the current king was known to be.

The king transplanted noblemen and their family members to lands and estates in the northern part of England, near York. He even placed a few of his very loyal nobles up there as well. However, the more of his followers that he placed up there, the more supplies he needed to take care of them, until their own farm lands began to produce enough food. In the southern part of the country, the greedy king tried to impose more taxes on the people, but they had nothing to give. The wars with France that this king kept them in were bleeding them dry to the point that they didn't have enough to feed their own families. However, that didn't stop the king from taking what they had anyway. If the farmers on the king's land wouldn't give what they were 'taxed' to give, they were either run off or killed and then the king would replace them with someone more loyal to the crown than themselves.

So when the people were unable to pay, he would run them off or have them killed and then he took their lands. He replaced them with more nobles loyal to him. It was a vicious circle that seemed to have no end.

One area the king was having a big problem with was this particular area of Scotland. The Scottish was alienated when a Roman emperor built a wall in northern England. As much as the emperor was trying to upset the Scottish with this act, he failed and they were actually not all that mad about it. They wanted to be a country all their own and they didn't want to be ruled by that or any other tyrant that was bent only on dominating the world, or at the very least their little corner of it.

So he decided that he would transplant one of his closest nobleman right here in what is now called Stewart Castle. The nobleman that he chose was a God fearing man named Audric. Audric is an old Gaelic name which means wise ruler. It was a name that seemed to suit him because he, after only a short time, had earned the respect of the people.

He was well liked by the people because he was fair and just. This was different than the way the king he served ruled. The knights that served as protection in the area liked him. He was one of the rare nobles that actually earned the respect of those in his area and did his best to keep it that way.

He and his wife had four children, two sons and two daughters. His oldest, a son William, stayed in the south with the king as a part of the knights serving the crown. His youngest, also a son, Edward wasn't old enough to join the knights but told his father frequently that once he was old enough, he would follow in his brother's footsteps. This saddened Audric, as the legend goes, because his sons wanted to follow the ruthless, greedy king more than their own father. The nobleman lived his life as a man of God. He knew that he couldn't hold his sons back but in his heart, he prayed they would see the king for what he was and that their hearts would change.

Audric had two daughters, Denalla, which means dark haired elfin girl and Aileen, and that is where the story really gets to the heart of the heart of the matter, no pun intended.

Denalla was a strong woman and this made her father and mother very proud. Audric would be heard frequently saying that he never had to worry about his children because they all knew how to take care of themselves.

One day, Audric was walking through the courtyard of the castle grounds and he noticed that Denalla was standing with Sir Aylwin, one of Audric's most skilled knights. At first he was furious that the knight would be so bold as to speak with his daughter. It was inappropriate and unheard of. However, his anger turned soft when he heard his daughter laugh at something the young man had said to her.

Days passed and the two were seen with each other whenever they could. They never hid their affection for one another. When Sir Aylwin approached the young lady's father to ask for her hand in marriage, Audric was extremely impressed that he respected not only him, but also his daughter, so much so that he would do such a thing, the legend says that the two men walked near the edge of the loch, this loch, right about where we are at right now when the younger man asked for the beautiful Denalla's hand in marriage.

Audric knew that as his daughter grew up and became even more beautiful many more men would try to win her affection. He believed that this young man standing in front of him, next to the loch, was a good man, a worthy suitor, and would treat his daughter well. He had been a part of his garrison of knights for the last few years. Sir Aylwin had been respectful and when the times called for it, did his duty and protected the nobleman and his family with his very life in danger.

With happiness in his heart, Audric gave his blessing to the young couple and agreed that they had found the best match for each other. As they walked back to the castle, the news had spread already and the locals were all rejoicing that Denalla and Sir Aylwin were going to be wed. Denalla's younger brother met the two men in the courtyard and also gave his blessing on the union. Standing on the edge of the courtyard were, Denalla, her sister and her mother, all beaming from ear to ear as they had anxiously waited to see if the elder nobleman would give his approval.

It was about six months after the wedding when Audric received word that the king of England was requesting that each nobleman in the north send his top five best knights to go and fight for the crown.

There was a growing war as some of the clans from the highlands of Scotland that were trying to win their independence. This infuriated the king because it was showing his foreign enemies that he was at war with as well, that he wasn't strong enough to rule his own entire land.

Audric knew that his daughter wasn't going to be happy when she found out this news. Sir Aylwin and Denalla were newly married and had already begun their family. Denalla found out earlier that week that she was with child and like most first time parents. Soon she would learn that her beloved husband was going to head out to war.

Sir Aylwin was one of the best knights that Audric had known. The young soldier had served the nobleman for a few years at that point. He was confident that his son-in-law would be fine going off to battle and returning back. However, he wasn't sure that, as strong as she was, that his daughter would be just as confident. The caring father's fears were soon realized when one day the three of them were out walking near the loch.

Audric was broken hearted when he heard the news. He didn't want to lose his best knight but even more than that, the last thing he wanted was to see his daughter separated from the love of her life. He was at an impasse on what to do. Sir Aylwin was in the large hall when the dispatch riders had brought the news. They knew who the best knights in the area were so there was no way he could lie and say that his son in law was dead or injured.

The king's messengers left the castle to head on to the next stop on their list, with commitment from Audric that his men would arrive within one week. The nobleman took his son in law to the side to discuss his options, few as they may be.

Audric had a quiet dinner with his wife, daughter, and son in law that evening to discuss options even though he knew there really was only one. Sir Aylwin had no choice and everyone sitting at the table knew that he would do his duty. The nobleman was very proud of his son in law, even though Audric knew that this quality about him would break his daughter's heart.

The day that he left was a sad day throughout the area. Most of the people were there to watch as the horses were loaded and the knights prepared to leave their loved ones behind. Denalla's little brother was one of the men that was chosen to go with the group. Audric knew that this was his older son's doing and this infuriated him even more at losing both of these to the greed of the king. With the exception of Denalla's little brother, the men riding with Sir Aylwin, who was the captain of the guard, the lead knight, had only been a part of the garrison of knights for only a short time. Sir Aylwin had never been in battle with them but if his father in law trusted them, then he would. In that very moment though, the only thing that Sir Aylwin had on his mind was that all this was breaking his wife's heart.

Just before he was about to mount up on his horse, Sir Aylwin walked over to his beautiful wife who was standing less than five feet away with her parents and her sisters watching the saddening scene unfold. Sir Aylwin took his father in law's hand and gave it a firm shake. Audric wasn't going to settle for that and embraced the young man who had stolen his daughter's heart and told him that he was proud of him. He gave a glance to his younger son and said that same thing, but the younger man just turned his head away, not returning any of the sentiment that his father had offered. The nobleman's younger son went to his horse and waited for the order from the captain that they were to depart.

Sir Aylwin went down the line of family and then finally arrived in front of his wife. He pulled her close with his arms tight around her. Her tears were still on her face as they continued to embrace. Just before he let her go, he whispered something in her ear that no one standing around was able to hear.

While her husband was going to fight a war that no one really understood beyond the evil greed of the king, Denalla would go to the church to pray for the safe return of her beloved. Her faith and that of her husband, in God was more than just ritual. She fully believed in the Heavenly God and Father of her Lord and Savior Jesus. The lovely young noblewoman knew that the only way that her Sir Aylwin would return safely was by the grace of God. If he didn't she knew that he would be safe in His arms until they were reunited according to his plan.

The day came when she received word that her beloved Sir Aylwin had fallen in battle. Most people would have taken that news and gone into such painful mourning, that they wouldn't have survived it. The legend goes that she immediately went into the church and Audric made sure that no one bothered her until she came back out. Less than two hours later, she did. There were no tears. There didn't seem to be any sorrow. A strong woman walked out and went about her new life as she was supposed to."

It is rumored that the strength she felt was from a story in the bible when David lost his child and was praising God. David knew that his child was in heaven and that there was not going to be any more pain for that young child. He had put his faith in God and no matter the outcome he would not let his faith falter. Denalla was trying to do the same thing. So every morning, after she would eat her small breakfast and tend to their child, she would go off to the church with the little one in tow. She would spend a good hour in there praying and giving thanks for the child and the short time she was able to love more than she ever thought she could. There, waiting outside of the church door, were a few rose bushes. She would pick a rose from the bush, carrying it down to the water of the loch and throw it in. The waves would take the flower and carry it off into the mist.

Audric was impressed with the strength that his daughter showed during the time she mourned the passing of her husband, his son in law. He knew there was nothing he could do to bring him back to her but if there had been a way, he would have surely done it. One day he was talking with his daughter and his grandson near the loch. Audric asked his daughter what he could do to honor her husband. He turned and looked across the water and asked what the name of the loch was. Denalla didn't know as she believed they had never given the loch a name. Her loving father suggested they name it Sir Aylwin. Denalla was not fond of it. Then the idea hit him. We will name it Loch Grádh. I have never witnessed more love between two people than I have between you and your husband. You two set such a good example. The family loves the two of you as do the entire people in the surrounding area. You are right, Sir Aylwin, isn't the right name, Loch Grádh is the perfect name.

From that day forward this body of water had been named, Loch Grádh, meaning 'lake of love'. Denalla was very thankful to her father for the love that he showed her.

True love isn't measured by what is gained but rather what is given, that is, how much of yourself are you willing to put into making it survive. The love between Lady Denalla and Sir Aylwin was a rare kind of love. It shouldn't be rare but sadly it is.

~~~~~~~~~~